One Day THE Wind Changed

Also by Tracy Daugherty

FICTION

Desire Provoked: A Novel

What Falls Away: A Novel

The Woman in the Oilfield: Stories

The Boy Orator: A Novel

It Takes a Worried Man: Stories

Axeman's Jazz: A Novel

Late in the Standoff: Stories

NONFICTION

Five Shades of Shadow: Essays

Hiding Man: A Biography of Donald Barthleme

One Day
Wind Changed
THE

Stories *by* Tracy Daugherty

Southern Methodist University Press · Dallas

Copyright © 2010 by Tracy Daugherty
First edition, 2010

Requests for permission to reproduce material from this work should be sent to:
Rights and Permissions
Southern Methodist University Press
PO Box 750415
Dallas, Texas 75275-0415

Cover photo: "Path to the Wormhole" by Jared Revell, Melbourne, Australia
www.jaredrevell.com.au

Jacket and text design: Marisa Jackson

Library of Congress Cataloging-in-Publication Data

Daugherty, Tracy.
    One day the wind changed : stories / by Tracy Daugherty. — 1st ed.
        p. cm.
    ISBN 978-0-87074-559-1 (alk. paper)
    1. Southwest, New—Fiction. I. Title.
    PS3554.A85O54 2010
    813'.54—dc22
                                                    2009052923

Printed in the United States of America on acid-free paper

10   9   8   7   6   5   4   3   2   1

For Margie, and Hannah, and Joey

The desert is in the heart of your brother.
—T. S. ELIOT, "THE ROCK"

Contents

Acknowledgments

It has been one of the privileges of my life to have a long and steady working relationship with Kathryn Lang, Keith Gregory, and George Ann Ratchford of SMU Press.

I am grateful to Marjorie Sandor, Ted Leeson, Ehud Havazelet, and Glenn Blake for their careful reading of some of these stories, and to Bob Fullilove's keen eye during the copyediting.

Some of the stories in this collection first appeared in the following journals: "Purgatory, Nevada" in *Southwest Review*, "Very Large Array" and "Temptation" in *The Hopkins Review*, "Magnitude" and "Bern" in *The Georgia Review*, "The Sailor Who Drowned in the Desert" in *Fairy Tale Review*, "Shopping with Girls" in *Northwest Review*, "The Saint" in *Prairie Schooner*, "Closed Mondays" in *Boulevard*, "The Leaper" in *Triquarterly*, "The Republic of Texas" in *Green Mountains Review*, and "The Inhalatorium" in *The Texas Review*. I am grateful to each of the editors. "The Inhalatorium" was reprinted in *Best of the West 2009*, edited by James Thomas and D. Seth Horton.

"Observations of Bumblebee Activity during the Solar Eclipse, June 30, 1954" is a variation, with additions, on a scientific treatise by Astrid Loken from *Publications from the Biological Station*, edited by Hans Brattstrom, University of Bergen, 1954.

Purgatory, Nevada

It was Stephen's last night in the Doom Town. Final check. Crickets chirred in the brittle yellow brush beside the streets. He thought of that Lorca poem—how did it go?—*The boy was looking for his lost voice. / The King of the Crickets had it.*

Stephen inspected the sidewalks, the storefronts, and the awnings. He glanced up Main Street. The bank. The public school. Wouldn't Sherrie love this place? It was paradise.

But Sherrie was back in Texas. It was clear from that first day, as soon as the men showed up, that she wouldn't come with him.

Stephen walked over to the school, made sure the main door was locked, and remembered the building he'd been working on when the black sedan pulled up, the men got out and asked for him. It was an elementary school in Brazoria County, south of Houston, on the edge of a large rice paddy—crowded beyond its capacity with the kids of low-wage workers. The school district had hired Stephen to design a few new classrooms, a more usable space. They'd given him a budget of twenty thousand dollars.

To cut costs, he had doubled the functional role of almost every structural element. The light diffusers also diffused the heat; he built the corridors to a larger-than-usual scale to make play areas for students. He clad the exterior in a glass and marble curtain wall. Cheap. Efficient. Just what he'd been hired to provide. And he'd come in on time.

All of which had favorably impressed the federal government, according to the men from the car. The government had been looking for an innovative architect: how would he like to design an entire small town in the Nevada desert?

They knew their man. Despite Stephen's exemplary work habits, and his fiscal responsibility, his practice was stymied because he had developed a reputation among contractors as a son of a bitch. On every job, he insisted that builders test each weld. Time-consuming, yes. But you couldn't risk being sloppy and having a roof fall on kids. If someone failed to meet Stephen's window specifications, Stephen made him rip out all the frames. Only reasonable, he thought, good and careful work. But word got around. Demanding. Obsessive. Next thing he knew, he couldn't get a steel bid anywhere in East Texas (and steel was *already* scarce, because of the war).

The men from the car were well aware of the economic maelstrom about to engulf Stephen. They knew he needed a break, a change. More importantly, they understood how much he wanted to be appreciated for his exacting eye to detail.

"Detail is what we seek," said one of the men. They both wore gray suits and black patent leather shoes. Friendly and calm. "Right down to the door locks and the window latches. *Exquisite* detail."

The catch was, no one would live in Stephen's town. It would exist to be destroyed. A military test.

"We want to see what happens to certain woods, emulsions, bricks, glass, and paint," said one of the men, "to locks and latches, when . . ."

"When what?" Stephen asked.

"Various possible scenarios," he answered.

"How can you even consider it?" Sherrie asked Stephen that evening at home. "You've been trained to *create* buildings. To make humane, livable spaces for people."

"It's just a job. And a fascinating challenge," Stephen said.

Streamers and balloons from their New Year's Eve party two nights ago littered the living room. Giant cardboard numbers taped to the dining room wall spelled out the date—1945. The books, Stephen's Christmas gifts from Sherrie, remained on the living room coffee table. Lorca, Kierkegaard—his most cherished authors. They were difficult to find in English. He was touched that Sherrie had gone to such trouble to order the books. She said her efforts earned her the right to tease him. He was an "elitist," she insisted, a man who read Europeans whose names no one could pronounce. "You're an arrogant son of a bitch," she added, laughing.

"I like them for the structural exactitude of their sentences," Stephen said.

Sherrie hit him with a pillow and wrapped him in streamers. They had often talked of traveling to Europe, learning Romance languages so they could read important poets and philosophers in their native tongues (when pressed, Sherrie, a high school English teacher, confessed to elitism too), but Europe was in flames, and it wasn't likely they'd get there any time soon.

Or at all, Stephen thought, strolling down the alleys of the Doom Town. The night she'd pummeled him with the pillow was the last time they'd laughed together. Once he accepted the federal commission—designing a ghost town in advance—she turned away from him, as though families had actually lived in this unrealized community, and he was responsible for their slaughter. "Our country is at war," he argued over breakfast, his last morning in the house. "This is a patriotic act."

She shoved the Christmas books into his arms and locked herself in the bedroom. They'd been married less than a year—a whirlwind affair based largely, Stephen feared, on Sherrie's idealized admiration for his work: making the world a finer place by organizing better, more comforting spaces for people (admittedly, he had bragged of this during their courtship).

Well. Her view of him—her ideals—had been shattered. What could he do? A job was a job, and this was a special assignment at a crucial time. Historic. He was certain no architect, anywhere, would have turned it down.

Would she leave him now? Return to him after a period of punishing silence? He couldn't tell, anymore than he could tell how the war would end. Finally, people were unknowable, in public *and* in private. He peered through the windows he'd dreamed into existence, into the dark, empty spaces inside the buildings. What kinds of lives might have played out here, in another time, under different circumstances?

He emerged from the mouth of an alley and glanced proudly up the street at his school. Inside the building, he had showcased the ventilation ducts, placing them in the ceiling, out in the open, rather than hiding them within the walls. This had the effect of breaking up broad surfaces inside the rooms, reducing the sense of mass. He had specified that the walls be painted off-white for reflectivity and airiness. One of his better designs.

Tomorrow morning, it would be obliterated.

A sand castle.

The week he'd arrived in Nevada, a man who described himself as a "low-level official"—they *all* described themselves that way, just as they all wore prim gray suits—let him in on "a little secret" (Stephen had gone drinking with him in a Vegas casino one night): Stephen's town, he said, was a test-run for a scheme cooked up by the Allies. A firebombing. "The idea is to drop bombs of such intensity—say a cluster of four-pound thermites—in areas with high concentrations of structures, so fires will break out rapidly, very close together, superheat the city, and force a rush of hot air upwards—a tornado of flames."

"So what you're telling me is that, essentially, you'll burn the air?" Stephen said.

The man nodded. He ordered another drink. "We think of it as liberating the city."

He said plans were in place to target a spot in Germany. Dresden, perhaps. The small scale of Stephen's town wouldn't predict every outcome, but the test would give strategists odds on what they might expect.

Sand castles, burning. "I might as well save you the trouble," Stephen told his low-level friend. "Design a moonscape. Cut to the chase. Craters. That sort of thing."

The man said nothing. He didn't smile. A keno runner, collecting cards, hurried past the bar where they sat.

Charred lungs. Flesh. Stephen shut the images out of his mind, and joined his companion in a second drink.

He walked across Main Street, now, to the central park—one of the few open spaces he'd been allowed to design. His clients wanted density, plenty of it. Fuel for the fire. He sat on a bench. A purple and orange dusk. The King of the Crickets sang to him: a faint and cheerful insistence in this land of final reckonings.

Stephen imagined Dresden. With Sherrie, he'd studied photographs of the city in travel books on Europe. Once a medieval marketplace, full of palaces and fortified walls along the River Elbe, now it was a lively *neustadt* of art museums, statues of heroes, glittering monuments.

And after a firestorm? A roar that would never cease. Rubble, smoke, and waste. People running from flaming interiors, unaware that the air itself was scorched.

Stephen closed his eyes and listened to the cricket. His beloved Lorca—a victim of the madness in Europe. Well, perhaps it was a mercy the poet had died so soon.

Sherrie was right, Stephen thought. I *am* an arrogant son of a bitch.

Tomorrow morning, his work would lie in ruins: its finishing touch, a badge of success. He would return to his motel room in the little town of Purgatory, twenty miles away. One of the low-level guys might fetch him for a drink, or suggest they drive into Las Vegas to see the newest additions to the Strip: The Meadows, The Pioneer, The Last Frontier. Ray Anthony and his Orchestra, featuring the singer Kathryn Duffy, played every night now at the El Rancho, with its freshly paved parking lot and the neon-lined Dutch windmill on its roof. Plans were afoot for the most glorious casino ever, The Flamingo, reportedly financed by mob money (a rumor that greatly amused the government men).

Vegas was already ruined. The bomb would improve it. "Ah, come on now, you got no sense of humor, no fun?" the officials said whenever Stephen made remarks along these lines.

He had read somewhere that the desert had once flourished underwater. Then, over eons, the marshes receded, the rivers slipped underground, the mastodons vanished.

The cricket went silent. The sun was gone. Up and down the avenues—his sweet little streets—corner lamps began to glow. Soft, ghostly lights. He rose from the bench, pulled from his back pocket the small notebook in which he made sketches, his studies of ideal perspective, and began a letter to Sherrie:

> Dearest,
>
> Somewhere, Kierkegaard says that life can only be understood backwards, but it must be lived forwards. Looking back now, just a few months, I assure you I understand everything, *everything,* differently.

It wasn't true. The truth was, he understood nothing—not while the world roiled and lurched.

Nothing is what they'd paid him to produce. In detail.

Nothing would be his legacy. *That* he understood.

He tasted dust. The wind kicked up. He closed the notebook and returned it to his pocket. He walked across the street to the school. One of the side doors, next to the auditorium, had a small hole in it, just above the lock, a consequence, perhaps, of clumsiness on the part of the builders as they installed it. He'd speak to the contractor in the morning, he thought—then he thought, What's the point?

This door was hollow-core, cheap, a last-minute addition, lacking the loving detail of the rest of the project. Just three days ago, he'd received instructions to finish the town early: the test had been expedited. Optimal weather in Europe.

Stephen slipped inside the school auditorium, to a storage cabinet in the back of the room. From it, he removed a toolbox and a small block of foam insulation. He wasn't one of those architects who lived in his head, inside the cages of numbers they'd sketched on the page. He sought hands-on action—another sore spot between the contractors and him. He smiled. His expertise around the house was one of the things that had first endeared him to Sherrie.

Returning to the damaged door, he filled the hole with foam. Though working in the dark and in an increasingly bitter wind, he managed well by taking his time, making sure his movements were exact. The door creaked as he pushed and pulled it. With a razor blade he sliced away the excess material, then, with a putty knife, he spread vinyl spackling on the patch. In half an hour, when it dried sufficiently, he'd sandpaper the surface of the door and touch the whole thing up with paint. He stepped back. Splendid.

Very Large Array

"You want boredom, go sit in the center of the universe," he said. He cut into his blood-rare T-bone. I finished my coffee. Sturling's was empty except for the two of us and a pair of middle-aged Navajo women chattering over chocolate ice cream in the corner by the kitchen. It was after ten p.m. Each night now I stop by the diner for a mug of decaf and a slice of blueberry pie to fortify myself for the late milking. Occasionally I bump into an impatient young genius—an astronomer working with the radio telescopes a few miles down the road at the Very Large Array.

"And what's with the local motels?" he said. "At the VLA I can pick up radio waves from a gas cluster millions of light-years from here. But at the Beechnut Lodge and now over at the Meadow Wind, I can't get squat on TV—and the signal's from Albuquerque. Eighty miles! Last night I tried to make it through an old Jimmy Stewart western, but Lord, the noise and the snow . . ."

It's an impressive getup out there, off Highway 60. Twenty-seven giant antennae looking like some spook-set from a Hollywood movie. Visitors running around arguing about molecular clouds, magnetic fields. Their skin broils because they spend their lives under fluorescent lights and they show up unprepared for the desert. Star-guys. You'd think they'd understand about the sun. "The center of the universe," they call it: the Very Large Array, its ears pointed at the Big Bang, listening for God's salty sigh (surely, by now, the Almighty would be weary, bleached-out, and salty; I imagine his breath smelling like desert sage). But for the visiting scientists, who've applied for observation time on the 'scopes, the VLA experience is apparently less than stellar: all night in a tiny, carpeted cubicle monitoring computer screens, sipping soft drinks, trying to stay awake (ceiling fans purring to keep the instruments at a moderate temperature), watching for errors or distinctive data. Most of them—and this young Einstein, last week, was no exception—are more excited that Sturling's offers 32-ounce steaks for under five bucks. I've learned you get what you spring for—especially with Sturling—so I stick to the pie.

"What's your project?" I asked the guy. Nothing these Brains ever spill makes sense to me. I don't know a fucking thing. But I figure it's best to treat strangers kindly in case someday I find myself a stranger somewhere.

"Young stars," he said. "Where, in the Milky Way, most of them form. At McDonald Observatory last year I did an infrared survey on a supernova remnant, IC-443, and found a dense cloud in that arm of the galaxy that might be a star-cauldron." He sipped his water. "The VLA can determine if there are fainter young stars embedded in the cloud—*if* we get the damn equipment straightened out. Right now, Antenna 11 is out of commission. Pointing problems."

He was thin, this fellow, but I could see that twenty, thirty years under crackling lights staring at screens was going to soften and settle him into something like a pudgy human anthill.

"Young stars. You mean, like—"

"Origins. Birth. The birth of everything. Nothing comes from nothing. What do *you* do?" he said, polite but only half there.

"Rancher," I said, checking my watch. "And the Holsteins are waiting for me." As I rose to leave, I caught the chill I often feel at night when lights burn low and people get scarce. Cold space wafts between my body and the nearest living thing, and I think about my parents, gone now, because nights with them in the old house by the hearth used to be so pleasant, and I remember Liz, my wife, recently passed—leukemia, the doctors said, but I saw she was done for the first time I showed her my two and a half acres and she glimpsed her hard life, whole, like a signal from the future—and standing there, as I so often do, in Sturling's, I smelled the sage that always fills my nose in lonely moments. I don't know why, an odor from nowhere, from God, I guess, if I believed in God, a collective dryness across time, smudging the years away, piling up like tumbleweeds against an old cistern after a dust storm.

I turned at the door and saw that part of what I'd sniffed—the hard mustiness—came from the folds in the clothing of the Indian women, the red cotton blouses and woolen shawls. They'd risen from their table, a few paces behind me, their faces whiskered with ice cream melting into wrinkles, exhaustion, and mirth—this last because they're also accustomed to the weekend whiz kids around here. "Saw a *snake* out back," one of them hissed at the hungry young astronomer.

"Oh?" he said.

"What's your name?" she said.

"Nick."

"Nick, this snake was curled up like a rope set to snag a grizzly. It was eating its tail."

"That's a myth," he said. "I mean, snakes don't do that."

"Where you from, Nick?"

"Manhattan."

"Ever been out to the desert?"

"Not this desert."

"Then you can't say what's being born here and dying, can you? And you know what else, Nick?"

He set his bloody knife on his plate. "What else?" he said.

"Little by little, that snake is going to swallow itself." She adjusted her shawl on her shoulders: a stark, earthen pungency. "Then its jaw will turn inside-out, and when it does . . ." She made a snap-shut motion with her left hand, then her right. " . . . the universe, the whole damn shooting match, will *blink out!*"

Her friend howled.

"Ancient wisdom."

"Right," Nick said. He looked at me.

In the doorway, a light breeze chilled my neck. "Can't help you, Nick," I said. "I've lived here all my life, and I don't know a fucking thing."

A smart kid, he fell back on certain knowledge: people always want something and it's easiest to give them what they're after if you can. He reached into his pocket and offered each gal a handful of coins.

"Thank you, Nick, thank you!" Snake Woman said. Her friend laughed again. "When you vamoose, now, don't go 'round behind the building. Just leave that critter alone to do its hard work. May take ten years, or a hundred, or a thousand or more, but we don't want to rile it, now do we?"

The ladies slipped past me, out the door, smelling solid. Permanent. *Geologic.*

"This place," Nick said, "bores the shit out of me."

Look harder, I nearly said. *Listen close.* Instead, I muttered, "Good night. Have a pleasant stay," and walked out under clouds and no stars, a smell of sage, a whiff of faraway mountains (a mixture of snowmelt and granite), and a low, persistent absence from nowhere I can name, like a small, tenacious weed in the Sangre de Cristos—a weed.

Valley Winter

Meteors let go past the sliced moon in the pockets of a dark, pulsing thunderhead. No one can say how long it will rain.

It rains on the chopped stalks of a field by a road where Okies broke their backs in '36, bent over berries, peas, and nuts. It rains on the shack where picked nuts once were kept; where winter wheat waits this evening to dry; where a white man and a brown woman made furtive love, just once, in '42, and never knew each other again.

Okie. Chicana. Two worlds passing like falling stars.

It rains on rows of seedlings touched by few wet hands, now that gears and grease and oil rule the land. These days, the woman's grown son trails a tractor every spring, picking up gravel, scrub, debris. The man's legitimate son, the one he'll sometimes bother to acknowledge, has never met this older brother, never even heard of him, or known that his father had a tryst before his marriage. He has inherited the old man's work, and owns the factories that make the tractors in the fields.

Tonight, it rains on separate paychecks, on the worlds they will—or will not—buy. It rains on tinted bank windows, crumbling public housing, this soaked and weary crowd we call our town: people whose families touched years ago, a shy miracle in the shape of an unlikely couple, an unpredictable union—happy, unthinking, relieved—one hot, rainy day in a shack after work, where no one gave a good goddamn, just as, tonight, we're all past worrying how long it's going to rain.

Magnitude

E ach week, here in the Dollman Planetarium, we host children's tours. Fifth and sixth graders. They burst through the door full of questions.

"Does the sun make noise?"

"Does Saturn wear bracelets?"

"Do clones have belly buttons?"

As I watch the kids' faces, I wonder who among them will grow up flummoxed by the world. Over there: the boy with the blue backpack, bumping into walls, chasing sun rays reflected off his teacher's watch—yes, a possible dreamer. That quiet girl sucking her thumb, picking her nose . . . her withdrawal suggests she can only sip at the world a little at a time.

The kids delight in the handwritten letters framed on the walls in the hall outside the Star Room. Astronomers from all over Texas, particularly from McDonald Observatory in the mountains down south, receive strange and hopeful notes from people. Sometimes the astronomers forward the letters to us and we display them, with permission from the writers or their families. I love to help the children sound out words, or wend their way through especially prickly sentences.

Today, three tall boys gather before Ms. Ruth Simon's letter, addressed simply, "To Whom It May Concern / McDonald Observ." The boys' teacher, a thin, redheaded woman with an alluringly high voice helps them read it:

Gentlemen:

There are holes in the sky, if you know where to look. Sometimes you can stare through them and glimpse the nations of Heaven. Heaven is industrious and efficient, and its citizens are busy plugging the holes so we can't see in. This is not a malicious effort—they know we would be utterly bereft if we saw too clearly what is beyond our grasp. Still, it is your duty as scientists to expand our knowledge, even into the areas God deems forbidden. You must hurry. I suggest you train your cameras and 'scopes on Lyra, now, tonight, before the angels spackle all the gaps.

The thumb-sucking girl stumbles through A. J. Rymer's note to NASA from the early 1960s. It is framed in red-stained oak. She presses her face to the glass and mouths:

If you ever get up there, please know that the moon is pure pumice, straight from the earth's core. I have proof, and I don't need the Bible for this, that Earth was once much bigger than it is at present, but it busted apart upon collision with some unholy solar debris. The Bible doesn't say so but I can prove this is accurate, if you would like a demonstration at my home (I'll be gone next month, but anytime after that is fine. Tuesdays, around three, are best).

The girl turns to me. "Is this true?" she asks.
"No."

"Then why is it on the wall?" She aims a wet thumb at my face.

"Because the man who wrote it *thought* it was true, and it's interesting to look back, with what we know now, and see how ideas change or grow."

She squinches her nose. Freckles like cinnamon. "If it's not true, it shouldn't be on the wall."

Ah. A seeker of answers, a hugger of absolutes.

"Are you the man who makes the moon rise?" she asks.

"Yes."

"Do you live here?"

"Not exactly, no. But I'm here much of the time." *Too* much of the time, my lover said last month when she walked out on me, leaving behind only a Tupperware container full of tofu and, in the bathroom trash can, a frayed black bra with straps as thin as garter snakes.

One of the girl's classmates, a pudgy boy with unlaced sneakers, stands behind her, staring at the sign

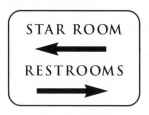

as if unsure of his needs. Body or soul, young man. Stir yourself.

"I think it would be neat to live here," the girl says. "It's always pleasant and warm, but you think you're outside when the stars are on. It would be like camping out in a room."

"Yes, it *is* like that, a little."

"I'm Anna."

"Hello, Anna. I'm Adam."

"I know." She points at my name tag. "It's a very nice name."

"Thank you."

The teacher—Ms. Pickett, I hear the kids call her—tries to gather her class at the Star Room's entrance, a curved, blue-painted portal with a velvet curtain. "People! People!" she says, waving her hands. "The show's about to start." The lilt in her voice—a charming, almost-whistle—reminds me of a Mayan flute. The curator of our sister institution, the Dollman Natural History Museum, once removed such a flute from its case, after hours, when the two of us sat in the building sharing a bottle of scotch. Last year, before the museum was closed, we commiserated over gutted budgets and the trustees' pressure on us to provide more "upbeat" shows.

The flute, made of clay, was as hard as petrified wood, but it sang like the wind. Its sweetness echoed down the museum's dark halls. We raised our tumblers, quoted ancient poetry, and toasted history's delights. Now the building is shut, and Bowers, the curator, a nice if drifty fellow, has moved on.

Frank Wilkins, chair of the Board of Trustees, warned me that the solar system could be packed up as quickly as the Indians if I didn't do something soon to attract bigger crowds.

Whistle, Ms. Pickett! Call the scattered children. Will you be my siren, my gorgeous pied piper? I'm healthy (relatively), young (relatively), early forties with a bothersome wheeze. Still, if you don't look too closely—

But she's wearing a wedding band. Overworked and harried. No doubt she has money woes of her own, at her school.

The constellations tell amazing stories of rescue. In today's show, I'll point out Aries the Ram and inform the children how, in Roman mythology, Phrixus and his sister Helle escaped his black-hearted stepmother on the back of the beast—but for me, this fine day, no savior.

Listen to me. My thoughts always race before a presentation. It doesn't matter how often I've addressed the public. This afternoon, I'm edgier than usual because last week on the phone Frank mentioned he might drop by before today's show. I know what's on his mind, and I don't want to talk to him.

The kids settle into their seats. It's clear who the poor, friendless children are, slumped and silent, like my friend Zero whenever *he* shows up (thank God I haven't seen him today). I blow into the microphone to test it. A low hiss: the cool mistral, cycling in from the north, stirring memory, stirring ghosts . . .

A pair of brothers wheezing at night, listening to the wind on the plains, reading to each other (adventure tales, ancient myths) when they couldn't fall asleep, and two loving parents who served as their compass points. Viewed from the bedroom window, the stars were our steadiest companions, because, asthmatic, we couldn't play outdoors without losing our breath to the dust in the air.

I remember, one morning, walking to church with Mother and our grandmother. The sky was red with dirt from the roads. Marty and I had to stop to use our inhalers. Our grandmother was temperamentally unhappy, her frown never greater than when she praised the joys of the Lord. Watching us struggle, she said to our mother, "How did you manage to raise two such damaged kids?" Immediately she apologized for the remark—miserable old woman—but Mother was in no mood to accept her regret. We didn't make it to church that day.

That evening, Mother stood with Marty and me at our bedroom window. Marty fought me for space. "Get back, you little creep!" he hissed. Mother made peace between us. She taught us a funny saying, to recall the names of the planets: "My Very Educated Mother Just Served Us Nine Pickles. Remember those first letters, okay, and you'll know your way around." She told us the sky was a wondrous bazaar, full of goods we could buy if we saved enough coins.

"How much does the moon cost?" I asked.

"And the sun?" Marty said.

"Five cents apiece," Mother answered. She pointed at a cold red star in the south sky. "A ruby ring. And that yellow one? Saffron, to spice up our food." The Milky Way was a fan of peacock feathers, she said. It was hard to take my eyes off it. Behind us, my bedside radio played a quiet tune. The horizon was flat in all directions. "You are the very best boys," Mother whispered, her voice as pretty as the music. She kissed us each on the ear. "Don't listen to your grandma, okay? Sometimes life isn't fair. But you know what?"

"What?" Marty said.

"You've got each other, right?" Sometimes she sounded as corny to me as the song lyrics on my radio, but that didn't matter. I loved her *and* KOMA—"*Stay right where you are! You've got the* Voice *of Oklahoma City!*"

"And you know what else?"

"What else?" I said.

"You can have anything you want. Just wish for it." We scanned the sky until our father came into the room to tell us a bedtime story.

My story today, tailored especially for the children, touches on distance and time. I'm ready to draw the curtain and start the music (what would stir the teacher, I wonder—piano solos, a rousing march?) when Frank, always punctual, walks in the door. He motions to me. "Excuse me," I tell the kids. "Back in a flash. In the meantime, why don't you try to locate yourselves using the directional markers at the base of the dome—north, south, east, west. That way, you'll be oriented when the sun sets." They stare at me as though I've greeted them in Chinese.

In the hall, Frank shakes my hand. He's a wiry man, mid-fifties, still fit but a little worn: pencil-line wrinkles below the bushy ears, thinning eyebrows, a hairline hard to find precisely. He's a real estate lawyer in Dallas. As a boy he was a stargazer—his happiest memories, he says. His mantra, since becoming chair of the board, is "State-of-the-art. State-of-the-art. We need to become a state-of-the-art institution." *And* be fiscally strict.

Frank plants his feet in front of the interstellar shots on the walls, just to the left of the handwritten letters. He rubs his chin. "Scratch Pluto," he says.

"Frank—"

"Kick it out. It's a piker. An imposter."

"All their lives, people have been taught that Pluto is a planet," I argue.

"Well, it's not."

"Not everyone agrees with that conclusion."

"The boys at the Rose Center say it's a rotten little—"

"Ice ball, I know. But the International Astronomical Union—"

"As you're aware, Adam, the Rose Center is the country's premier planetarium. Absolutely state-of-the-art. From now on, it's the standard by which we measure ourselves."

"Frank, with all due respect, there's no way we can compete with the Rose, or anywhere else, on the budget of *pretzels* you give me. Since when is *science* the board's business? You're supposed to watch the purse strings. That's all."

He folds his arms and speaks to me as if to a child. "Adam,

we've been mandated, by the Dollman family, to oversee the health of this operation. And in the board's estimation, we need to be perceived as a crack educational facility. If the nation's state-of-the-art planetarium says Pluto's a bit of space trash, a snotty little rag God blew his nose on—"

"More like the ice in his scotch."

"—then that's the way it's going to be."

I understand that this is just a minor annoyance for Frank. But I know my audiences. Like children with their bedtime stories, planetarium visitors insist on familiarity and repetition. They need to believe that their universe is steady.

"Frank, correct me if I'm wrong," I say. "Last week you told me our priority was entertaining folks, even if it meant cutting back on the hard science. Keeping them happy—"

"Right."

"Believe me, then, what'll keep them happy is the comfort of knowing that their parents and teachers told them the truth."

"We need to be taken seriously, Adam. Our profits depend on it." In its oak frame, the Andromeda Galaxy swirls behind his left shoulder. Dear Andromeda, chained to the rock of economic forecasts. "We're going to try one last Sunday ad in the *Morning News* this year, quarter page, trumpeting our cutting-edge vision—*and* our special half-price midweek shows."

"I see. So, on the one hand, we're supposed to be a circus, and on the other, the National Science Foundation."

"You got it."

"You're asking the impossible."

"And you're just the man to do it!" He pats my arm. He wasn't on the board when I was hired. I'm not the person he would have tapped for the job. Before leaving, Bowers heard rumors, which he happily passed on to me: Frank has confided to his colleagues that he finds me an "odd duck," a "damn loner."

"I've got kids in there," I say. "I shouldn't keep them waiting any longer."

"Anyway, what's the problem, Adam? Just change your show a little. It's not the end of the world."

"I'm fond of Pluto."

"Forget it. It's an outcast."

"Exactly."

"Tell me." He grasps me by the elbow and pulls me close: a stiff, fatherly gesture. A curious mix of intimacy and power. I know what's coming. He likes to be the wise old sage, and often gives me advice in the name of professional solidarity. This forced bonhomie must be a ritual lawyers practice to keep from killing each other. "Wouldn't you be less . . . *exercised* by these matters if you had a family at home?" Frank says. "Someone to spend time with, take your mind off work? I mean, I love work. I put in twelve, sometimes thirteen hours a day, but when I'm done, I'm *done*, you get me? Shoes off, stiff drink. Wife purring beside me. See what I mean?"

"Thanks for your concern, Frank. It's much appreciated. But I manage." I think, How does God do it? All alone; bedeviled by petty demons; all those burned-out suns to replace.

"All right. It's just that *your* health is the board's concern too, you know," Frank tells me. "You're our front man here, Adam. Got to stay strong. In the breach, eh? Anything you need, you come talk to me, hear?"

"I need more money and a clearer direction, Frank."

He sighs and throws up his hands. In the doorway he stops and turns. "By the way, Adam?"

"Yes?"

"We're not a homeless shelter, okay?"

So. He's seen Zero. He's seen the others. My cheeks burn.

"It's up to you to encourage the *right kinds* of crowds. All right? Think 'families.' Think 'wholesome.' Have a good weekend. Get out and have some fun."

Funny, how running a planetarium—with its self-generated months, years, light-years—compresses my sense of time. After over three decades, my most vivid Saturday remains the one when I was seven, and my mother drove me into Oklahoma City from our home in Holdenville. We were going to see the Beatles in *A Hard Day's Night*, a rare treat. My mother didn't like rock 'n' roll, but the Beatles, she said, seemed "wholesome."

Marty had no interest in music. He went to the oil fields with Daddy that day. Daddy had to check on some rig production.

I remember sitting in the plush moviehouse—bright lobby chandeliers, silver spigots on the soft drink machines, crushed velvet curtains by the screen. It was nicer than anything I'd ever seen. It smelled like a new car, leathery and polished. I held my mother's hand. When the Beatles began to sing, every hair on my body (not many back then) leaped to attention. Music and light—from that moment on, their twinned power has stunned me.

I'd never witnessed four young men happier than the Beatles. In the middle of the film, when they broke free of their cramped rehearsal hall and scampered, like puppies, through an open field— when they ran, as Marty and I never could—I thought I'd faint from pleasure. My breath caught in my chest. Mother looked at me, worried. I reached into my pocket and gripped my inhaler, but I managed to settle down and didn't have to use it.

After the show, in the car, I hugged my mother, hard: her belly's soft heat through her pink cotton dress, the fluff of her breasts against my cheek. She took me to an ice cream parlor for a chocolate sundae with candy sprinkles and nuts. Sunlight shattered off my spoon onto her pretty, lipsticked smile.

The parlor was near my grandmother's house, and I asked Mother if we were going to see the old lady. She smiled and said, "No, this is our special trip. Just you and me, okay?" The ice cream tasted sweeter then. Our special trip! I sat up straight in my wrought-iron chair. "Why is Grandmother so unhappy?" I asked.

"She's had a hard life," my mother said. "Life is hard here on the plains."

"How?"

"Are you kidding? All this dust and heat. Nothing but oil field work or farming."

"Do *we* have a hard life?" I asked.

She laughed. "What do you think?"

"I think it's all right."

"Me too."

Through the parlor window we watched the sun set. The evening star appeared above a mud-brown line of dark, one-story buildings. "Make a wish," my mother said.

With Frank gone, I draw the curtain to the Star Room. The velvet has frayed at the bottom. Mental note: New velvet. Bypass the board. The children are laughing and talking, throwing sharp paper triangles across the room. The kids' clothes smell like spoiled milk. Ms. Pickett shakes her head at the pudgy boy I'd seen in the hallway, the one with the unlaced shoes. He's begging to go to the bathroom now. I've dawdled and made the teacher's job harder than it needs to be.

"Hey, Adam."

Damn, if it isn't Zero, slouching in the back of the room. Apparently, he slipped in while I was chatting with Frank. *Slipping in* is Zero's best skill.

"Hi. Come in. Sit down," I say. "We're about to start."

He looks around. His real name is Robert McCleod, but I call him Zero because of his fascination with Nothing. He's mildly schizophrenic, and forgetful about his medicine. In fact, he prefers to self-medicate. Vodka, mostly.

"What's the show today?" he whispers.

"Just an intro kind of thing. For the kids."

"Uh-huh." He rocks back and forth on his feet, the way he always does when he's nervous (when is he ever *not* nervous?), the way he did when he first confided in me. It was late one afternoon. I was cleaning the room after a lengthy performance, a show Frank attended "just for fun," he said, but I felt sure he was there to evaluate me. Zero had lingered until the crowd was gone—did Frank spot him then?—and I noticed this strange fellow watching me. He looked a bit like my brother, lean and wiry.

Unbidden, he began: "One morning I forgot to bring my pills to work." I was startled. He cleared his throat. For a while, he had worked as a file clerk in a suburban police department, he told me. "I was sorting fingerprints and, a little dizzy, I noticed how they all looked like big fat zeros. Our fingerprints are supposed to be unique, keys to our individual identities, *comprende*, but it struck me, man, that we're all zippo. Zilch. Goose eggs. The prints don't lie."

He didn't seem dangerous, but I couldn't be certain. He lingered by the curtains. I gripped my broom to my chest. Evidently, he mistook my silence as encouragement to go on. "I tell you this because I figure, as a scientist, you'll appreciate it," he explained. "Eventually, the police department fired me for misplacing records." For Zero, this marked the start of a quest to find the original Nothing.

Now, between odd jobs, he spends his days at the main branch of the Dallas Public Library, poring through books or microfilm, or he comes here, trying to get his "mind around the empty center, the pre–Big Bang." "The Sumerians made zeros, pressing the tips of hollow reeds into wet clay tablets, which they preserved by baking," he told me one morning. "This is the first record we have of man's awareness of Absence." The Natural History Museum had already closed by then or I would have sent him to Bowers. Now he's attached to me. I give him books to read on the nights he can't sleep, yellowed volumes I've picked up in secondhand bookstores, or old things Marty and I used to share. I listen to his troubles.

I ask him, "How are you today, Z?"

"People been messing with my *stuff*, man. Stuff's been disappearing lately."

Paranoia: a bad sign. He must be off his Stelazine.

I haven't saved his place. Usually he doesn't show up on Fridays when the schoolchildren do. The boy with the backpack has grabbed Zero's favorite spot and refuses to budge. M&Ms won't do it. Nor will a dollar. "I *know* the stars," the boy tells me, pointing to the big blue **N** beneath the dome. "This is north, right? Don't try to fudge me." His fingers are sticky with something. He wipes his hands on the seat. Little creep. You need someone to keep you in line, I think. A stern granny, perhaps, or a big brother pissed at the world. "This is the best place to see Polaris, and I aim to see it," the boy tells me.

Zero whips off his Texas Rangers baseball cap and scratches his thin brown hair. He's twenty-five, with an adolescent's acne and the balding patterns of middle age. "Adam, man, I got to have my *chair*," he whispers, rocking furiously now. "It's the only place I can see the quark!"

Quarks are Zero's latest kick—an obsession he's indulged for a couple of months now. After the Big Bang, he says, matter and anti-matter almost annihilated one another, but there was one extra quark in a corner of the universe—a flaw in God's plan to perpetuate a perfect nothing—that tipped the balance toward messy creation. Inexplicably, the day he ran across this concept in the library, he saw a seagull downtown, a rare sight in landlocked Dallas. He took it as a sign that he was onto something.

His breath smells of alcohol. Ms. Pickett scowls at me. The children are getting restless. "Zero, you're going to have to try a different perspective today," I tell him, steadying him with my shoulder. "Try this seat. Just once. I'll bet you'll see nothing at all. Won't that be a treat?" He settles warily next to Anna and fumbles with his cap. She picks it off the floor. He snatches it from her hands. "You're welcome," she mutters, then jams a thumb into her mouth.

I make my way to the console, passing Ms. Pickett. "I hope you enjoy the show," I say.

She fidgets in her seat. "Thank you."

"Do you know the stars?"

"A few."

"Then I'm happy to expand your universe."

She frowns as if I've made an indecent suggestion.

Zero trembles in his seat, his cap pulled low across his eyes. Anna stares at him. The chairs creak and shift with age. The dome is stained with water spots. Rain doesn't fall often in north Texas, but when it does our firmament suffers. Three or four pesky leaks have resisted all repair attempts. But when the lights dim, and the false stars rise, the dome's skin, the dome itself, vanishes behind illusory depths.

I press a yellow button on my console to prepare the music. Glenn Gould's version of the *Goldberg Variations* is a favorite of mine—soft and sedating, but with a sure mathematical precision. On other days, depending on the show, the airy gaps and mysterious instrumentation of Brian Eno's *Music for Airports* encourages wonder and a spooky anticipation among the crowd.

I flip a switch. A small gray stone, pierced through its middle and attached to a nylon pulley, shoots noiselessly across the horizon. A tiny meteor. No one sees it but me. It's the one part of the show that I perform for myself, and I always start this way. The stone dances, free, across the heavens, past the illusion of clouds.

I lower my lips to the mike and welcome everyone to the Dollman Planetarium.

The Big Bang, I came to call it—the awful humor of the phrase offered me a kind of comfort. Or maybe it provided a distraction. One weekend, two months or so after the explosion, I drove to Oklahoma City. I had just started work at the planetarium. Clouds and birds wheeled above me.

The Murrah Building's remnants had already been razed.

At Northwest Fifth and Robinson Streets, I circled the chain-link fence draped with teddy bears, strolled around the YMCA and the Water Resources Board. The buildings' windows were boarded, walls pockmarked and clawed. Glass squeaked beneath my feet.

Flying ants filled the still, humid air. A toddler with her mother reached for a yellow ribbon on the fence. Above the ribbon a sticker said, "Proud to be an Oklahoman."

I tried to picture the damaged soul who had conceived of such a wasteland and then carried out the attack (of course I knew his face—but only his face—from the news). What had time done to him? When did time *stop* for him?

"Cain't imagine one of *ourn* did this," said a man in a Peterbilt cap, strolling with a friend past the fence. His buddy said, "I don't believe it. It's a lie."

A man standing next to me picked a small gray stone off the ground. "Looks like part of the building," he said. "You know, I was in there the day it happened." His eyes misted. "Damn lucky to be here now," he said. He nodded at empty space. Was he on the level? I didn't know what to say to him. Before he wandered off to talk to others—a Flying Dutchman of the Heartland—he dropped the stone into my palm. Instantly, I imagined it hurtling through space. I looked up. My hand brushed his, just slightly.

Dusk is a red button at the top of the console, sunset a silver lever next to the music's volume knobs. The sun sinks fast or slow, depending on the show, the crowd's mood, or my whims. At the dome's base, representing the horizon, a scale model of the Dallas skyline, with buildings that light up at my command. It gives viewers a sense of the sky's immensity, stretching over our city.

Well. The buildings are *supposed* to blaze. Faulty wiring keeps plunging my tiny Dallas into darkness. The tip of Reunion Tower is missing, the result of an overeager janitor swiping at cobwebs with a mop. One night he broke off the lighted ball and we have yet to find it. This year, the trustees have cut our maintenance budget, so now *I'm* in charge of the spiders' handiwork.

On the north side, the perforated-aluminum dome has warped in the heat, our air conditioner being unreliable. This blemish leaves the impression that the Milky Way near Draco wobbles a bit, like soap bubbles. In the south, a small aluminum panel has peeled away from the surface: a jagged edge pricking Scorpio's heart. The universe looks a little ragged.

Our newspaper ads tout us as one of the finest educational and entertainment attractions in the Dallas–Fort Worth area, but we're failing. Our equipment is outdated. Crowds have dwindled, except on school days like today. We're unable to offer people the extravaganzas that blockbuster movies, laser light shows, video games, and computer simulations have primed them to expect. The trustees have begun to question the efficacy of continued advertising. The Dollman family, who seeded our initial endowment three generations ago, has long since ceased to concern itself with our daily operations. Macrocosm on a shoestring.

But I'm proud to have secured my regulars. Since becoming the program director five years ago, I've built a small fan base.

No. No, that's incompletely true.

The fact is, a handful of lonely souls, un- or underemployed, finds our Star Room a more congenial refuge than diners, park benches, or their own stuffy apartments. They drop by when they have nothing better to do, always gravitating toward the same chairs. If I think one or more of the drifters may appear on a particular day, I try to save the seats. "Excuse me, ma'am, I think your children might have a better view over there," or, "I'm sorry, there seems to be a draft on this side of the room today. Try *that* row."

Affectionately, I think of Zero and the others as my "comets."

Like space's errant ice balls, they're *slushy* inside, unstable, forever circling a void, always coming back around, drawn to me or my shows as Halley's or Hale-Bopp is pulled to the sun. Or perhaps they recognize me as a social castaway too. "Darling, what's so *hard* about fitting in?" my mother used to ask me—years, even, after I'd graduated from college. Astronomy excites certain sensibilities, I told her: minds attached to symmetry, vast numbers, philosophy, or transcendence.

Obsessives. Dawdlers. Dreamers, flummoxed by the world.

Almost every morning seems the same now, as though time has halted. This morning I stalled, as I do every day, while I unlocked the planetarium's big glass doors. I noticed sparrows gathering on the ground by the remnants of the old Natural History Museum. It's shuttered now. Beside it, in a dirt patch, a stack of two-by-fours lay under a wrinkled blue tarp. An art dealer has purchased the place and plans to turn it into a gallery.

A United jet hummed overhead, lowering its landing gear, heading for DFW, a few miles north of here. Thirty miles or so to the east, the Dallas skyline glimmered, green and gold, in the early morning light. From my vantage point, the city appeared no bigger—and much less uniform and pleasing—than the toy city ringing my dome. A second plane passed. It looked like a sparkling silver skate key. The fields smelled of creosote and sage. Green smells. Black smells. Brown.

I remembered, then, as I stood with the keys in my hand, last night's dream. With minor variations, it was the same dream I'd had the night before. I was standing in a field very much like the one behind the planetarium. My father, wearing overalls and a green Mobil Oil cap, was lying in the charred ruins of a granite building. He got up, dusted himself off, and walked up to me, over broken, tinted glass. He was grinning. I took his hands. They were chalky and cold.

"Father—" I said.

"All I wanted was my social security check," he said.

"Father—"

"Your mother and I walked in the door . . . it was a beautiful morning in the city, remember?"

I whispered, "You didn't make it, Father. I'm sorry."

"Oh." He looked at his body, then back up at me. "Are you in touch with your brother?" he asked.

"Yes. Sometimes."

"How is he?"

I shrugged.

"Neither one of you . . . you just couldn't seem to *grow up*. Why not, Adam? Why did you *stop*? Was it your breathing? Never had many friends. I worried like the dickens about the two of you."

"I know," I said.

"And you—always trying to hold firm, keep things steady. You can't do that, you know? Hell, you *do* know that, son, don't you? You must."

"Yes."

He turned, walked back to the ruins, and lay down again among the blackened stones.

Before the kids arrived with Ms. Pickett this morning, I sat and watched plane after plane after plane angle for the airport. I watched the sun glide behind clouds (sloppy clouds, irregular, thick; in my sky, they would never, never do).

◉ ◉ ◉ ◉

Stepping to my left now, behind the console, I check the dissolve control on the slide machine, then the projection orrery, which will illustrate the motion of naked-eye planets around the sun on the dome. I reposition the meteor projector, then lower the A3P so it will display tonight's sky, at our latitude, at approximately ten o'clock. The star ball buzzes faintly, a mosquito whine, as it moves. Now we're ready for Glenn Gould.

I dim the cove lights. Piano runs unfold, soft as whispers over the earthy thrumming of the bass notes. Anna watches me closely. I catch her eye and point to the east, where a hot air balloon made of cardboard and newspaper clippings hangs over miniature buildings. I fashioned the contraption, and fastened it with tape and slender wires over Dallas, after reading about an eighteenth-century architect's cenotaph design: a huge, empty ball, illumined from within to resemble, alternately, the night sky and the sun. He wanted viewers, while contemplating death, to find themselves "as if by magic floating in the air, borne in the wake of images in the immensity of space." The idea, he said, came from watching the Montgolfier brothers' balloons, the first hot air balloons to sail over Paris, just before and around the time of Manet. Anna smiles at the funny blue sphere.

It's when people are around, and I first nudge the sun with my controls, that I'm most aware of the dome's bleak and toneless color, a cool ceiling over all of creation. Alone in here at night, I relish the lifeless vacancy of my space, its beautiful, mechanical boredom that puts me at ease. It demands nothing of me. It doesn't need my help.

The star ball is like the jar I used to carry as a kid, with holes punched in the lid to keep captured fireflies alive, only *this* jar, the

A3P, contains all of the flashing galaxies. Everything ordered and neatly tucked away until I release the universe, its edges blurring above us, the Star Room becoming the same size as the cosmos. *Becoming* the cosmos. I take us through an entire day in two minutes. The children's T-shirts burn with fluorescence. Yellow, blue, green spill from the Dallas skyscrapers, then flicker and quit. The bad wiring. My jaw clenches. I want my city bright and safe. Measured, with clear and manageable paths.

As the sun winks out, a poetic fragment—Baudelaire—skitters through my mind: *declining daystar, glorious, without heat and full of melancholy.* The children gasp at the blackness, then "ooh" as they start to perceive the stars, which are about the size of nail heads. I'm always light-headed at this point, aware that the sky is being cast from below, onto a solid barrier above, then I lose myself in the illusion.

I think of the boxes of Joseph Cornell. I have a book at home, with pictures of his lovely, dizzying art. *Toward the "Blue Peninsula"* is a simple white container filled with wire mesh. Behind the wire, a tiny window opens onto startling blue sky—a glimpse of infinity in a claustrophobic space. *Cassiopeia #1*, only fourteen inches wide, its inner walls plastered with star charts—heaven folded into the equivalent of a cigar box. But most delightful is the *Solar Set*, a box featuring sketches of the sun, and of Earth's orbit around it, behind five fluted glasses, each holding clear yellow or shadowy blue marbles—phases of the moon. Glass on glass. The delicacy of Order. Totality, held like a caught breath inside a small, sealed case.

Somber whole notes. Minor chords. "Nature is an infinite sphere whose center is everywhere and whose circumference is nowhere," I say softly into the mike. I'll bet Zero is smiling in the dark. He brought me this Pascal quote, and I always use it when

he's here. "I'm your host, Adam Post." I fade in the moon. A ficti-
tious evening. Time governed by my sure, pale hand. "The planetarium is a vision generator. There is nothing it cannot
demonstrate. So sit back, relax, and enjoy Existence."

The kids squirm. I show them the major constellations, tell
them the story of Aries. I give them dimensions, sizes, distances.
Explain the ecliptic, magnitude, orbits. Retrograde motion.

"Excuse me," Backpack says. "What's magnitude?"

"Intensity of light—the way we measure it."

Someone pops a gum bubble.

I show them the planets as they'll appear tonight in the sky.
"The ancient Maya of Central America had no telescopes, but they
tracked stellar movements," I say. Cue Venus. "What we often call
the evening star is really the planet Venus, and the Maya based their
584-day calendar on the time it takes this bright sister of the earth
to cycle around the sky. The Maya associated Venus with the god of
rain. At their latitude, the planet's absence was shortest in the dry
season, longest during showers.

"Now, many of you have probably memorized the phrase 'My
Very Educated Mother Just Served Us Nine Pickles' as a mnemonic
device—that is, as a way of remembering the names of the nine
planets in our solar system. If you take the first letter of each word in
that sentence, you can recall the planets in the order of their orbits
around the sun: Mercury, Venus, Earth, Mars, Jupiter, Saturn,
Uranus, Neptune, and Pluto." Pause. "Recently, scientists have
debated the nature of Pluto, and many now contend that it's not a
planet at all. They say it's composed of ice rather than gas or rock."

Faint stirrings. My eyes have adjusted. I see Zero stiffen.

"This links Pluto with a ring of icy bodies beyond Neptune
known as the Kuiper belt."

"But that's not fair," Anna says quietly.

"Anna?" says Ms. Pickett, with her warm, melodic voice, "do you have a question, sweetie?"

"It's not fair that, just because it's made of something different, it doesn't get to be a planet. Is it?" In her voice, I hear the accusation: *Little creep.*

"This isn't unprecedented," I say, glancing at Ms. Pickett. Trust me, my eyes say, I didn't want to follow this path, I wanted to keep things just as they were, but . . . "The asteroid Ceres was once counted as a planet until other asteroids were discovered, and its true nature could be understood."

"We studied Pluto just this week, and the books all said . . . I'm confused . . . are astronomers certain about it, or are they still deciding?" Ms. Pickett asks. "Anna raises an interesting point, I think."

Believe me. I'm just the man to resolve the impossible. But how? "A consensus has yet to emerge on the scientific definition of 'planet.'"

"But now it doesn't mean anything," Anna says. Her face is deeply flushed, even in the dark. The death of an absolute. Hard to bear. Her freckles glow like embers in the fake green moonlight. "My Very Educated Mother Just Served Us—what? Nothing. She served us nothing!"

I look at Zero, thinking this might perk him up. He shivers, removes his cap, loses his grip on it.

"The Kuiper belt is a swarm of ice—" I say.

"It just isn't fair!"

"Thousands of slushy masses, far from the heat—"

"No fair no fair no fair!" the kids all start to chant.

Ms. Pickett frowns, as if I've knocked the heavens out of whack.

Anna's foot brushes Zero's cap. She picks it up. He tugs it from her fingers. His eyes are wide. Now he rises. He covers his ears with his palms, turns to the group and announces, over the shouting, "Man presents himself as a being who causes Nothingness to arise in the world, inasmuch as he himself is affected with nonbeing."

Anna cringes. Ms. Pickett stands. The children get quiet.

I'm sorry I lent him, last week, my copy of *The Existential Moment.* But he'd said he couldn't sleep, and at the time it was the closest book at hand.

"Man is the being through whom Nothingness comes to the world. Thank you and good night."

"You're drunk, sir!" Ms. Pickett says.

He spins to face her and nearly stumbles into Anna's lap. Anna screams.

"Get away from her!" Ms. Pickett shouts.

He falters again. Five or six kids dash from the second row.

"People! People! Quickly! Come with me!" Ms. Pickett motions them toward the portal, as though the building were about to collapse. A scraping of notebooks, the roar of seats snapping up, milk-smell wafting through the not-alleys of Dallas. The kids' sudden motion jostles my balloon; it careens toward Reunion Tower. Mayday! Mayday! My lungs constrict. The Murrah stone zips back and forth on its string. Zero stands still, chin on chest; it's likely his brain chemicals have slipped off the charts. I've never seen him this bad. (What wastelands is *he* envisioning?) I'll have to take him outside, sit with him until he calms down. At least twice a month, we perform a milder version of this little dance and I'm always surprised at how quickly he circles back to—what? Normalcy? Steadiness?

"Please," I say, wheezing, but it's too late. Ms. Pickett won't look at me. "It's not the end of the world."

Oh, but it is. It is. The world is ending every minute. Just ask Z. Ask my former lover. The night she left, she held me and said sadly, "You can't save them, you know? Your comets? Your damaged friends? Adam, you can't undo things."

Ask Marty. "It wasn't true," he told me, the last time I saw him, in OK City. He held our father's Mobil Oil cap, recovered at the Murrah site. "Remember, Mom promised us? Anything we want."

"Well . . ."

"It *should* have been true. But I always knew it wasn't, didn't you?" He grinned at me. "Ah hell," he said. "It ain't fuckin' fair, is it?" He put on the cap, got in his car, and drove away from the missing building and from me.

"This way, people. Hurry, now, hurry," Ms. Pickett calls.

Teacher, Teacher, can't we clasp hands and watch it all crumble? Don't leave me here with nothing.

What's magnitude? Wheezing at night, and no one, no one comes.

Anna lags behind, gazing at the star ball. An instrument of betrayal. Faulty packaging for All-That-Is.

Of course, the board will hear about today. Reprimand? Warning? Frank has cautioned me that a few of the old gents have been seeking excuses to reroute the Dollman endowment, to use the money for more "commercial" ventures.

An "Out of Order" sign hung on the Big Dipper's handle.

"If it isn't fair, it shouldn't be done," Anna tells me.

Remarkable child. Where do you get this *shouldn't*?

"Is he okay?" She points at Z, who appears to be asleep on his feet.

"Not really, no. But I've learned how to take care of him."

"Good. Don't forget to make the sun rise again."

But it's the end of the world.

"Promise?" she says.

Okay. One wish, just for you. "Sure," I say. "Absolutely."

She nods, smiles, gazes up at the dome. Then she goes to join her friends.

One Sound

Night. The sea hugs the tip of the quay. In wind, a forgotten coat, stiff with salt, raises an arm to greet me as I pass. I'm far from the desert that made me, far from myself in sleepless longing for a woman. I must want to lie here on white stone turning colder with each new rush of spray.

Down the shore, unloaded boats bank off the wharf like desert horses rocking in their stalls. I must want to hear this and remember cowboys, drunk, hugging each other, a mare giving birth and biting herself, mad with pain.

Why did I think I could leave the flatness behind? Day after day, under a blank sky, neighbor girls hauled laundry baskets out under the webworms' silk, cracked pecans in the grass, laughing, stringing clothes between black trees loaded with little peaches. The trees just made it through each burning spring. All the while, my father washed his father with a sponge—the old man was dying, but slowly, year after year, softening like fruit.

Over and over (would he never quit, never live a life of his own?) Dad stroked the dry yellow skin, asked me, "Can you fill this bowl again—warm—for me, please?" Diesels whined on the highway out past the house, wind chimes rippled like water.

And tonight it's all one sound: the waves, the sucking of kelp, a girl's laughter from a misty, unseeable distance. I imagine her near, in blue light-panes from the boats, and tell her the whole long story of my love, my failure to get away: *He's put the old man to bed now. His father's whiskers float in the bowl of water; he pauses above me, thinking something I can't name. Outside, a foal is trying to stand.*

The Sailor Who Drowned in the Desert

The Sunday service had just ended. Father Thomas had prayed, again, for a budget influx to fix the sanctuary door, which was old and splintered with rusty hinges. The parishioners filed out of the church, through the cactus garden with its seven or eight ancient tombstones (one of them may have been only a rock—no one was certain, as all of the markers resembled rocks, with names and dates long since weathered away). Mrs. Latour gave an astonished cry, which stilled the crowd among the brittle pink flowers and the thorns. Attached to one of the tombstones, embedded deep into the granite, was a ship's anchor made of iron. A rope extended from a large ring at the tip of the anchor, where the rope was tied fast, and rose into the sky until its other end vanished.

Everyone stood aside and made a path so Father Thomas could approach the gleaming object. It appeared to be wet, though this was not possible; the day, like all the days in West Texas, was arid and dusty. The young priest bent to inspect the shiny hooks jutting out of the stone. As he did so, the rope rustled, went slack then pulled taut again as though someone in the sunny heavens had given it a good, hard tug. Father Thomas stepped back. The parishioners inched away toward the safety of the church (Mrs. Latour backed into a cactus thorn and gave a little "O!"). A little girl named Hannah, clutching her mother's skirt, said, "Listen!" Everyone stood still. From far above their heads came a low murmur like thunder, but there weren't any clouds, and the more everyone listened, the more the noise sounded like voices, perhaps half a dozen of them, concerned and trying to solve a problem. The rope continued to rustle.

Then Hannah said "Look!" and they all saw a young man, with wavy hair as yellow as the sunlight, clambering down the rope toward the anchor and the stone. He wore pants as blue as the sky. No shirt. His skin was the light brown of blowing dust in the late afternoon. He appeared to be struggling as he moved down the rope. It was as though an element dense and resistant slowed his arms and legs. When he reached the anchor he remained suspended, upside down, on the rope. He did not seem to notice the group, mouths agape, huddled around him among the flowers and the thorns.

From his pants pocket he produced a small silver blade. With it he began to saw on the rope, right where it was knotted to the top of the anchor. As he worked, he weakened visibly, his arm slowing, his grasp loosening on the coils of the line, his face turning blue. After only two or three minutes, and with little success in freeing the rope from the massive iron weight, he dropped the blade and fell to the ground. Dust puffed around him. The crowd backed away again. Again, Mrs. Latour pricked herself in the rear. "O! O!" she cried.

A tall old man stepped forward, out of the group. This was Dr. Alexander, who had delivered all of the babies in the parish (recently, there had been only two additions to the dwindling community—Hannah, now seven, and a boy a year younger named

Joey). Dr. Alexander pushed past Father Thomas. He knelt beside the fellow in the sky-blue pants. The doctor sniffed the air. Now everyone smelled it too: salt and brine. A blue horsefly buzzed about the doctor's head as he placed his ear to the stranger's chest, felt for a pulse in his wrist, and examined his eyes and throat.

"This man's lungs are filled with water," said Dr. Alexander. "He has drowned."

"Impossible," said Father Thomas.

"See for yourself," the doctor answered. He pressed firmly on a spot between the stranger's ribs. Water, green as seaweed, spurted from the young man's mouth. Everyone gasped as though each person, old and young, had developed breathing trouble.

Timidly, someone wondered aloud if this were an omen—of what, he couldn't say. Perhaps the cactus garden was sacred ground. It held the bones of desert pioneers. Who knows? The parishioners' heedless trampling of the dirt each week was an affront to God, maybe, and the spirits of these elders.

If so, why an anchor, why a sailor? someone asked. What did these things have to do with the desert?

Someone else suggested that the drowned young man might be a warning to the community that it was in danger of disappearing. After all, only two children had been born here in the last seven years; we are not being fruitful, we are not multiplying. We are getting old, all of us, and our good works will be swept away, with scarcely a ripple. Everyone agreed that this notion, however plausible, still did not explain why God had failed to speak to them through symbols more suited to the desert. A burning bush would be more like it, someone mumbled.

Then little Joey, the youngest member of the parish, squeezed past all the men and women, who stood planted, scratching their heads.

Joey held an open Bible. Almost from birth, he had been a precocious reader. His mother read aloud to him every night from the Old and New Testaments, and made him follow her index finger with his eyes as it glided past words on the page. "Right here," he said. "In the book of Genesis. God separated the waters above the firmament from those below." He looked up. "There must be a sea above the sky!"

Father Thomas stared at Joey with amazement and pride.

"Listen!" Hannah said again. Above them, the racket grew louder. Now, six wavy-haired young men, also dressed in blue pants and no shirts, came scurrying one by one down the rope. One gripped a small silver blade similar to the instrument the first young man had carried. Two others balanced between them a thick wooden pallet about the length of an adult male.

The parishioners gave them room. Should they rush to greet these glistening figures? Should Mrs. Latour run inside the church and whip up a big batch of potato salad for a hospitality luncheon? But the strangers, like their brother before them, appeared to be oblivious to the crowd. While the one with the blade hacked at the knot in the rope, the others attempted to fasten their drowned compatriot to the pallet, using hemp straps. After two or three minutes, their faces turned blue. They seemed unable to breathe. Finally, the rope snapped free of the anchor. It flew this way and that, as though tugged by an object in turbulent motion. The man with the blade signaled urgently to the others. They dropped the pallet. It thumped against a tombstone, raising dust, and came to rest against it at a forty-five degree angle to the ground. The strangers gathered their fallen comrade in their arms and hurried to link hands. The man closest to the end of the rope snatched the line as it began to rise into the air, and he pulled the others behind him until they had winked out of sight in the uppermost reaches of the sky.

None of the parishioners spoke. Mrs. Latour pulled a thorn from her flesh. "O!' she cried.

Silently, Joey pointed to the pallet, then he gestured at the sanctuary door.

Six years later, Dr. Alexander was the first of the old generation to die. Then Mrs. Latour. Father Thomas lived to the flinty old age of ninety-eight, and by the time he was ready to lay his body down for the last time, Joey was a vigorous middle-aged man—who called himself Joe—on fire with the words of the Lord.

As they passed away, one by one, the parishioners were laid to rest under sparkling new tombstones on a small rise overlooking the cactus garden with its flowers, thorns, and graying, weathered markers. Joe worked hard to maintain the fresh headstones, but sun and dust had begun, already, to wear names and dates off the square granite faces.

Hannah had married Joe's younger brother, who was born a year after the visitation of the sailors from the sky. Her seven children sang joyously each Sunday, and louder than anyone else, after Joe's sermons. The remaining elders said these were beautiful youngsters and, along with a few others born to families over time, were bound to produce healthy stock for the future. Each week, once the service had ended, the parishioners filed from the church, brushing their fingers across the solid sanctuary door, carved from the left-behind pallet, and the hinges fashioned from the hooks of the anchor. Every now and then, one of the men or women glanced up. Though all year the days remained arid and dusty, sometimes, someone said, the sky turned—just a little, over in the east ("Look! Look!")—the color of the sea.

Temptation

I've never left the desert. The serpent, still near, now in the shape of a diamond-back rattler, curls over black, eroded stones. He no longer tempts me to make fresh bread out of rocks. Instead, he tells me a fortune can be had in petroleum, but I'm not the least bit moved. I know the limits of the land. The pumps go up and down; their taut, metallic hammering drives right through my skull.

The roughnecks, knocking off for the night, toss their hardhats into the air, scattering skinny hounds in the road. The fellows head for the one bar in town, a small Texas town that remains a town just because Bubba's stays open. They laugh whenever they spot me. *Goddamn nutcase. Sees stuff that ain't even there. Thinks he's friggin' Christ, or something. Who knows, who knows? Rig broke, year or so ago. Conk on the noggin.*

I've heard much worse. Believe me.

Later, when Bubba's shut for the night, one wiry wildcatter stumbles to his trailer home, falls into bed next to a snoring woman. She wakes. They make love. I wait by their open window, tensed, poised to be useful if someone drunk or exhausted topples into a sinkhole here or burns himself in a gas-leak fire.

The couple coos. Their bodies cool. For a moment I'm only a jealous man.

Sensing my weakness, testing me, the snake hisses, "Take her. Just walk in and take her, man. Take it all. It's yours for the asking."

I love it all, it's true, and love means grasping, want, desire. But the value of the desert is its poverty. That's why I've stayed. And stayed . . .

Tonight, refinery flames outshine the moon, revealing lunar emptiness right at my own two feet. I'm reminded there's nothing here to claim: worn-out odds and ends. Behind me, a collie circles, dragging a hurt hind leg. I've seen him before, begging by the bar, abandoned like all of Earth's creatures, but he's never looked so stark. Ribs, muddy paws. He whimpers, as quiet as the sighing through the trailer home window. Now he falters, breathes into the dirt. I kneel, inhale the dust from his fur. *O how I miss you*, I whisper, *O how I miss you already*, but I mustn't sit with any single victim. Too many. Too many. Eventually, I'll be forced to leave him to the diamonds, the hidden flowers that open their mouths in the night.

On evenings like this (but aren't they *all* like this?), I tell myself again and again, a hammer in my head, I must live with myself, with only myself. I must learn to love what isn't mine, since nothing is mine. Nothing has ever been mine.

Shanty Irish

W as it the house, or what was happening in the house, that woke me, while tin bells sounded in my ears and dust pounded the window panes next to the clown in his big, brown frame on the wall?

My father had found us a three-bedroom rental on Hill Street, in a newly developed residential area near a power station and a row of Sinclair oil tanks. Our neighbors planted willows in their dirt yards, though these were poor attempts at trees. The wind carried dust and gravel past their leafless limbs and dumped them on our roofs each day. The tapping of pebbles on my window reminded me of poodles with pert, groomed nails prancing across a slick wooden floor, though where, at the age of seven, I had ever seen such dogs, or a wooden floor, I can't say.

Sometime after midnight, each night, I'd wake to the *tink-tink* of bells in the house—at the far end of the front hallway, in the kitchen, by the back porch door. Leather straps in bows tied the bells to my mother's fuzzy blue house shoes. *Tink-tink, tink-tink*, said the bells as she paced the darkened rooms holding my baby sister, hoping to rock her to sleep. Years passed before I registered the fact that the ringing always woke me, not my sister's bawling. At least where *she* was concerned, I seemed to have attuned myself to happiness.

Waking was not a welcome moment for me. Always, in the early mornings, dust-showers pierced the house. From the green wooden exterior to the foam insulation in the walls, ours was a house of dust. *Tink-tink, tink-tink.* I'd shoot up in bed, stirring, beneath the sheet, the heat-musk on my skin. Unfailingly, my first waking thoughts were of my grandmother, who had died of emphysema when I was an infant. I keep no memory of her death-rattle, though Mama swore to my presence in the room, writhing in her arms at the foot of the old woman's bed. Apparently, when Grandmother launched her last sigh, I determined that if *she* wasn't going to use more air, *I* would seize it. Mama said my eyes grew wide and I opened and shut my mouth, like a fish.

Now at night, in my father's house, I'd sit in the dark on my four-poster, listening for the window-scratching and the soft-stepping clarity of the bells. Seconds passed before I realized I wasn't breathing. Inside, my nose felt peppery—dusty and hot. I arched my shoulders and strained toward the ceiling. Up there, my father had pasted plastic glow-in-the-dark stars. I imagined I'd been sleeping in a canyon.

As I gasped, light-headed, stars flashed inside my skull—burst capillaries? ("capillary": a word I'd learned from my mother as she sat at the kitchen table over iced coffee, working crossword puzzles).

The sparks mixed into a single blurry presence: Grandma's ghost, coming to reclaim her breath. *Tink-tink.* She was gone. Had I really seen her? Or felt her or *something* in the room? A tapping at the window. Gravel. Dust. At last, air moved through me. Inhaling, I traced its sweet ache, crashing inside me like an ocean. I rocked with the happy rhythm, and my gaze came to rest on the clown.

My father had found him in *Life* magazine, in a photo-essay on the theme of running away from home—as in "to join the circus." The clown, in a green Irish leprechaun hat, smiled wistfully at the camera, but later, when my father reproduced his image in oils on a canvas, and hung it on my wall, the smile turned faintly malevolent—or maybe this was my child's imagination, for my father was a skilled, if untutored, amateur painter. I was delighted by the bullfrogs and finches and bluebottle flies he had rendered, as a youngster, on the backs of the bathroom cabinets in my grandmother's Oklahoma house. My father's imagined menagerie had survived the old woman, which impressed me with paint's scumbled power, so much stronger than the pulsing, soft organs inside us. Perhaps it was this feeling, inchoate but vivid in me as a child, that frightened me most about my father's clown. *This monster will outlive me.*

Each morning my father left the house and vanished in a veil of dust before he reached the end of the driveway (at least, this is my memory of watching him from the living room window—a small figure growing dimmer, as, down the block, the red lights on the power station's T-shaped electrical spires cut through the weak light of day). He may as well have flown to the moon. Would he ever get back home?

As soon as he left, my mother crumpled. All morning she wore her bathrobe. She wouldn't comb her hair. The bells rang on her feet as she breast-fed my baby sister and fixed me waffles. I attended school, though on many days asthma kept me in bed, and my most powerful recollections are of staying home with Mama, of shopping with her in the late afternoons, once she'd finally dressed.

While she pushed my sister in a cart inside the dime store, I'd ride the plastic pony by the door. It ate silver coins. It bucked up and down, like the oil pumps my father showed me once in the middle of the desert when I asked him what he did for work.

One day, my mother bought a vaporizer and placed it in my room: a round glass container, thick and green, brewing steam. "This will moisturize and cleanse the air," she promised me. "You'll breathe better." From then on, the vaporizer's hissing obscured the bells. I'd wake at night, feeling alone in the house, my breathing still rocky.

Mama must have cooked supper sometimes, but most evenings Daddy returned from his days downtown carrying bags of hamburgers or Chinese takeout from the Blue Star Inn. Once, my sister nearly lost an eye, playing with a chopstick while he prepared our plates. My mother scolded his carelessness, listlessly. He ignored her. Her misery with the house, the town—"Your boy can't even *breathe*!" she shouted one night in the kitchen—was so pervasive by now, I believe it was no longer, for him, one of her distinctive characteristics.

After supper, he'd ride me on his shoulders as he threw away the food bags. He'd stand in the alley behind our house, point at the stars, and tell me stories of the constellations: mythic quests, bears and dogs, seven secretive sisters. I didn't understand these tales, especially the stories of Greek or Roman heroes. Swords and pelts played no part in my desert life: the wait, each day, for Daddy to come home, for Mama to feel better.

We seemed a race apart, frailer, quieter than those around us. The neighbors were figures of great mystery to me. To the west of us,

the Casbeers, a father, two teenage sons. And the mother? In jail?
On the run from her men? Dead? What finally happened to mothers in the desert?

Papa Casbeer drove a big red truck and delivered oil field
equipment to rig sites. He wore green overalls and a baseball cap.
So did his sons. I'd see the boys at night beside the dirty truck in
their driveway, smoking and drinking from foaming silver cans.
The more they drank, the meaner their laughter became, and the
gravel of their voices, though I couldn't make out what they said. I
assumed it was beer they drank—"Beer" was part of their name, a
marked family!—and Mama said beer was bad for the brain. I
watched and waited for the boys to explode into insanity.

Sometimes they slipped inside their father's truck and started
the engine. They didn't drive anywhere.

On the other side of us lived Reginald Jones, a jolly bald man
who always wore aviator sunglasses and white short-sleeved shirts
with plastic pocket protectors. Reginald was a hero. He had raised
the prettiest girls in town, Ceci Jo and Jeannie. Their mother was
around too, but she was as squat and blunt as a leather suitcase.
Reginald was "no movie star," Mama said, but he radiated a deep
mirth and a vitality inherited by his girls. They were eight and nine,
too young for the Casbeer boys, but old enough for cultivation.
Whenever Ceci Jo or Jeannie walked up the street (wearing cotton
shorts and pink halter tops), the boys whistled and called, "Check
with me in five years, honey! I'll be here!" Always, Ceci Jo (or
Jeannie) shot back, "*That's* for sure."

Their teasing thrilled me, obscurely. After overhearing their
voices through the window screen, I'd jump on my bed as though it
were a trampoline. Then, wheezing, I'd stand with my face near the
vaporizer.

Reginald liked to drink "precisely one half-glass of beer before supper each night, to settle the nerves," he told my father. My dad was not a drinker, but occasionally he took a half-glass with his neighbor. Sometimes I'd sit at their feet, playing in the dirt. Sunset shattered across Reginald's bright amber shades. "Ah," he'd say, sipping his drink. "My soul is restored." He'd nudge my father's ribs. "I'm surprised you're not a tippler, old man. I thought you shanty Irish had a love of the hops." And he'd laugh.

The way he said "shanty Irish"—tossed-off and jokey—shamed and confused me.

One night, as my father tucked me into bed beneath the gaze of the clown, I asked him, "What's 'shanty Irish'?"

"Our name. O'Doherty," he said. "Our ancestors—your great-great-great-great-grandfather—and before him—came from a far-off place called Ireland. Green and pretty, with a wild, cold ocean."

"Have you been to it?" I asked.

"Nope."

"Mama?"

"Never."

"Would she be happy there?"

"Well." He pulled the sheet to my chin. "We'll have to work on her, won't we?" As he bent to kiss my cheek, I smelled the beer on his breath, and wondered if he'd hurt his brain.

When he left the room, I turned away from the clown. I settled into my imaginary canyon, breathed delicately, and waited to see if the bells would cut through the steam.

Not the *tink-tink* of Mama's shoes, but the clattering of a spoon on a glass. I sat up in bed. The jester grinned at me. Something at the window: waves of wind. The night wanted to add my body's air to its own. My breathing shallowed-out.

I threw off the sheet, placed one foot then the other on the cold linoleum floor. I crept down the hall to the kitchen. At the table, stirring sugar into a frosty tumbler of tea, sat a headless man in a business suit—one of my *father's* suits. I tried to scream.

Two nights later, I had another dream about my dad. I was sitting on the back porch watching him plant rosebushes by the house. "I don't think they'll grow in this soil and terrible heat, but we'll give them a shot," he said. "Your Mama'll like them." I glimpsed a black blur near my leg. A spider, no, a *tarantula* crawling toward me, getting fatter as it moved! I leaped up, screamed. It covered the porch now. Hairy. Writhing like an octopus. "Not to worry," my father said. He slipped past the creature, into the house, and returned with a double-barreled shotgun.

The threat in these dreams seemed part of the atmosphere of the house. A dusty penetration. My mother's emptiness had crept into my night life. What was the source of her misery? West Texas? Our home? Motherhood? My father's job? I didn't know. I'll never know. I loved her. I shared a house with her. I felt her despair like a presence in our midst. That's all I can claim.

My father continued to wear a cheery face, bringing food for us in the evenings, singing to Roy Orbison on the radio, trying to coax my mother to swing-dance in the kitchen (she wouldn't), and bringing the stars to life for me in colorful stories as we stood together in the alley. But I noticed that, more and more, he avoided whichever room my mother occupied. He no longer painted. His homemade easel (nailed together one afternoon in the driveway), his oils, canvases, and brushes were stored now in the back of a closet. In the past, before my bedtime, he'd turn the light on in my room so my ceiling stars would soak it up and glow for hours, once the bulb was out. Often, now, he forgot to do this. The stars remained shapeless, as though time had not yet commenced.

The lethargy that settled over our house made Reginald's vitality all the more attractive to me. "Shanty Irish!" he called to my father over the back fence one night as we returned from our trip to the alley. Supper was finished, but Reginald convinced my father to share a beer with him. "Let me show you my drums," he said, lightly tapping a beat on my back.

This was the first I'd heard of drums. On our way to his house, I also heard, for the first time, the story of Reginald's plane. Like Papa Casbeer, he hauled oil field equipment from Dallas to El Paso, but he did it in a Piper Cub, not in a filthy old truck. All at once, the words "oil field equipment" acquired an air of adventure I'd not linked to them before.

Reginald's house smelled of fried chicken. I'd never been here. Dark wallpaper, cross-hatched like Mama's word puzzles. An eight-piece trap kit sat in the middle of the living room, between two wooden floor lamps arranged like spotlights. In the lamp glow, the bright red drums sparkled like Dorothy's slippers in *The Wizard of Oz*.

Reginald brought my father half a glass of beer. Then he sat on the stool behind the snare drum and picked up a pair of sticks. Brushes—similar to my father's painting tools. Reginald kept his sunglasses on. "I looked y'all up," he said. He did a "slow Celtic march" with the hi-hat, the bass drum, and the snare. "In the library. The genealogy section. O'Doherty. You come from the north of Ireland. County Donegal. Rebels, warriors." The drumbeat quickened. A *tick-tick* on the large gold cymbal, the chiming of a bell. "The O'Dohertys were the last remaining tribe to resist the British before the shame of the Ulster plantations—one of your ancestors, a fellow named Cahir, sacked the city of Derry. That brought the Brits' blood to a boil, let me tell you." He laughed. "They came after him and *that's* when your family crammed into the shanties. I was right about you."

He varied the march-beat. Jazz and genealogy were his hobbies, he said. His family was Scottish. One night, in the downtown library, he had researched our name when his great-grandmother's trail dead-ended. "The thing I like about family history is it makes you bigger than you are, bigger than the daily grind. Like flying. The desert's a hell of a lot more impressive from above."

He thumped the tom-tom. "So, young lord." He looked at me, eyes hidden behind his shades. "Bet you didn't know you had the blood of rebellion in you, eh? Next time someone gives you guff, remember you're a warrior!" He offered me the sticks. "Take a turn?"

He was the warrior, I thought. The clan-lord. A sky-god.

A pilot. A drummer. A father of pretty girls.

On his right arm, a running-horse tattoo.

I glanced at Dad, pleading. Can I take the sticks? He shook his head.

"But Dad!"

The gentle tyranny of his frailty. *My* family's heroes have all passed on, I thought. Long ago. Nothing now but ghosts, hoping to suck us dry. "We should go soon," Dad said. "Baby girl back home . . ."

"How 'bout it, boy? Got a hobby?" Reginald asked me, grinning.

"No," I said.

"I took up drumming when I was your age," he said. "It's kept

me going, all these years. We all need *something*. You should try it."
He made the hi-hat hiss. "What about you?" he asked the slumping
shanty man in the corner. "What's *your* pleasure, old fellow?"

My father stared at his empty glass. "Oh. I paint, I guess."

As he spoke, Ceci Jo and Jeannie pranced into the room.
"There they are, the Scottish queens," Reginald said, staring with
frank delight at the beauty of his girls. He rattled a tambourine—
first against his knee, then on top of his big, bald head. I had never
witnessed such a *talent* for life. It embarrassed and excited me.

The girls slipped out the door, wearing tight blue shorts. My
father rose. "Okay, young lord," Reginald said to me. "Next time,
you'll play me a paradiddle."

"Thanks for the beer," Dad said. He stepped out under the stars.
I followed him. He was quiet. "What's that one?" I asked, pointing
to a constellation south of the Milky Way. He didn't respond.

"Dad?"

"Hm?"

"Why don't you paint anymore?"

"Oh, I don't know," he said.

"I think you should."

He laughed. "I thought you were afraid of my little jokester?"

How did he know? Had Mama passed my secret fear on to him?
How did *she* figure it out? It was my turn not to respond.

Laughter, low and mean, from the Casbeers' house. Where were
Ceci Jo and Jeannie?

I couldn't see a thing down the dark, flat slab of Hill Street.

We walked into the house. "I'm going to check on your mom,"
Dad said. "Get your pj's on, okay? I'll come tuck you in."

"Boys, is that you?" Mama called from the kitchen. "Where
were you?"

I heard my father sigh. My mother's voice rose.

Before I made it to my room I'd lost my breath.

In her crib, beside a largely empty bookcase in my parents' bedroom, my sister cried. I sat on my bed, glaring at the clown, waiting for someone to comfort the baby. I got up and toggled my light switch. A slow pulse—rebellious, steady, as glorious as a Celtic drumbeat. I told myself I was trying to ignite my stars. Would anybody see them?

Shouting in the kitchen. "Dusty," "ugly," "breath," like scattered clues from a puzzle. My father said, "Shh."

I went to my sister, whose face was puffy and red. From beside the bed I picked up my mother's house shoes. The bells rang. The baby hushed and watched me. Slowly, I waved the shoes, timing my shallow inhales to the beat I'd begun, recalling the firm movement of Reginald's fingers on my body earlier tonight. "Shh," I said. "Shh, shh, shanty girl. You're bigger than you think you are."

Wind rattled the window—seeking the last of my air. I sensed a shadow behind me. My sister laughed. Still shaking the bells, I drew the largest breath I could, and turned to look at my mother, my father, in the doorway.

Shopping with Girls

The trees and the fountain, along with the tinted glass and marbled granite of the storefronts, formed a small town beneath the transparent green roof of Westgate Mall. An idealized Main Street. Sitting in the regulated air (a constant sixty-eight degrees, Howard guessed), listening to water slap fake stones, he was happy to discover he could still feel desire.

If this was Main Street, it sure as hell belonged back east, Howard thought. The glitzy signs and the faceless mannequins in the displays were like nothing else he had seen in southwest Texas. He had courted Mindy on a typical West Texas street, twenty-three years ago. Walking home from the high school gym one October afternoon following a football pep rally, he had waited on the sidewalk while she ducked into Beasley's Shoes. Had he held her books? Probably, though he didn't remember. Junior year, 1975: chemistry, calculus, *The Red Pony?*

Every few minutes, she would tap the window inside the store to get his attention, lift slippers, pumps, or outrageously risqué red high heels, and seek his approval with her head cocked to the side, charmingly (she had built up to the high heel moment, she confessed to him later). In that brief ritual of the shoes, on that mild afternoon, he knew their future together. They would marry. Always, she would reach for the next dazzling thing. And he would wait on her and approve.

So how had he missed the fundamental fact: that one day she'd reach for the sky? He was an oil man. His world was prescribed, not in the clever way of the mall, with sales displays set in your path, bold colors used to inspire the impulse buy. No, Howard's world was defined by rotted organisms and the moraines in which they had died. Oil country was precisely circumscribed for a man with his rudimentary skills. In West Texas, he understood what to look for so detritus could be coaxed to the earth's surface for refining, packaging, and selling.

Outside this region he knew he'd be lost. So he kept his head down and paced the same old ground.

Petroleum's thick, jellied stink never did dazzle Mindy, except to repulse her. Finally, one year, dissatisfied with Howard and his desert world (it had been *her* world too!), she snagged a man from the clouds: a Boeing engineer. He whisked her off to Seattle, whose surfaces glistened with rainwater and looked twice as bright as they really were.

That October afternoon, twenty-three years ago, as Howard waited outside the shoe store, he looked up the street and spied in nearby windows transistor radios, portable hi-fi sets, chewing tobacco, saddle soap—none of which could be located today in the mall, just as none of the mall's treasures would have been offered, much less understood, on old Main Street. And back in the day, there were no unaccompanied women on the sidewalks.

He had felt fortunate, then, to stand near a girl who'd taken an interest, so much so that she'd adorned her feet to please him. That day, his approval of Mindy's footwear was his claim on her. Were he a high school junior now, he wouldn't dote on just one person (these kids and their freedoms!): he'd wallow in possibilities, the dreamy display of available beauties, alone or in small groups, all of whom wore tennis shoes or flimsy sandals: I can—and I will—fly away from you and back again into your arms.

O girls! O heart, O brain! I *am* still alive!

Moving toward him, toting a stark white Abercrombie and Fitch bag was a stunning young woman in a jeans skirt and black semisheer stockings, a beige sweater and a red silk scarf. She caught his eye and smiled. Young woman? No, a child, about his daughter's age. Twelve. Thirteen, at the most. Astonishing, the power of camouflage: lipstick, eyeliner, rouge.

And in fact, here was Alina now, with Meagan, her friend from Seattle. Howard hadn't paid attention earlier, but watching Alina in the cool light slanting through the leaves of the fat, potted trees, he understood that she wore makeup too: a moderate blush in the cheeks, a hint of blue on her eyelids (of course, she refused to wear her glasses in public). The more she tried to distinguish herself, the more she resembled every other girl in the mall—jazzed by the bills in her purse.

Howard chastised himself for lusting after girls his daughter's age, children testing their power, practicing sexy smiles, being adults. He stopped staring after Abercrombie and Fitch.

Meagan grinned at him, and he made a solid effort to return her greeting. He'd had trouble warming up to her, though it wasn't her fault: somehow, he linked her to Mindy. A slight resemblance? The same distracted air? Each time he had phoned the old girl, planning to get Alina home for a visit, she was on her cell, rushing around a fabric store or a furniture outlet, bargaining with salespeople. "Alina could bring a friend," Howard suggested to Mindy one afternoon. "She wouldn't have to fly by herself. Mindy, what if—"

"Yes, yes, the leather recliner," she said. "That red one in the corner."

In the world of her accumulated objects, there was little room for him now. "You're lucky she's moved away," Gary, a friend from work, assured Howard one morning in the coffee room, before they set out together to inspect a series of wells. "There's nothing worse than the Ex-Wife Dinner, those awkward meetings to plan for the kids or to split the medical bills . . . and always, afterward, out of guilt or whatever, you feel obligated to buy her an after-dinner drink or an ice cream or a little something for her bedroom dresser, which used to be *your* bedroom dresser too, so the two of you go to a shopping center and you sit there in the Baskin-Robbins or you walk around the jewelry store and things get friendly again, like the old days, warm and flirty, and you think, 'What the hell am I doing?' and you see she's thinking the same damn thing, and so pronto, you agree to call it a night and, I swear, *run away* from each other in the parking lot."

In the abstract, an Ex-Wife Dinner sounded oddly fun to Howard. Maybe with a different ex-wife. Better than finding in his mailbox monthly Xeroxes of Mindy's charge card bills with half the purchases circled in red. In her light scrawl, which he remembered from afternoons he'd copied her high school homework, the words "Alina's Expenses"—meaning, *You* pay, pal.

So: best to relax with Alina and her friend, and try to stifle his desires, as he had after Mindy's flight, when he'd paced more fiercely than ever the porous rock that cradled oil. *Oil*, which made it possible to build a mall on this site, this bright hormonal incubator . . .

"Can I have five more dollars?" Alina said, skipping up to his bench. Meagan stood behind her, still grinning, shy—distantly fetching, the way Mindy used to be.

"Why? What did you do with the money I gave you this morning?" he asked.

"We had sodas and a hot dog." Howard smelled perfume in the folds of her wool sweater: a bubblegum scent, faintly salty. "I want to look around some more, and I want to call Leann to meet us," Alina said.

Leann, short, pudgy, studious, and polite, had been Alina's best friend before Alina moved away. Howard had always liked her. He wondered if Alina's desire to phone her now signaled boredom with the mall—its boxy simplicity must pale next to Seattle's rainy wonders—or if it meant trouble with her new friend, Meagan. Maybe *Meagan* bitched about Texas, the crappy merchandise, Alina's grumpy dad . . . but he hadn't been so bad, had he? He'd sat patiently, letting them wander at will, and laugh and flirt with the laggard boys hauling skateboards around the fountain.

"You don't know what you want," he said, reaching into his back pocket for his wallet. "You just want to buy *something*."

Meagan giggled.

Alina snatched the bill from his hand. She pulled a cell phone from her purse. He'd bet the gadget matched her mother's (part of their "sisterly" pact since the family's split), sleek and blue, with a ring like dying crickets. "Thanks, Daddy," Alina said. She turned away and punched a button on the phone. "Leann?" she said. "Leann, it's Alina! Yes, yes! *Here*! In Texas, in the mall! Come meet us!" Meagan followed her, glancing at Howard with a tilt of her head, an unmistakably coquettish gesture. Half-closed eyes under wild, blonde bangs. He was startled by a splash from the fountain, a wet little kiss on his cheek.

The girls headed toward faceless figures draped in sweaters in the windows of Buffalo Exchange, with Meagan chattering to Alina about "guerrilla sewing—you know, like, cutting the sleeves out of my dresses and stuff. Really cool." Howard was saddened to see in Alina's skitter her mother's reckless movements, a dangerous approach warning others, I can't or I won't slow down, get ready. Or maybe it was just her shoes: tight, pink platforms that pitched her forward and quickened her pace.

Shoes—squeaking, sticking to gummy floors . . . Howard had a vivid early memory of shopping with girls: women, really, his mother and her sister. But they referred to each other as girls. "Girl, I don't know what to do with Howard," his mother sighed to his aunt on the phone. "He's outgrown all his shirts and his shorts are in tatters. I swear, he's a weed! We're going out on Saturday. Want to come?" And so the three of them marched up the same street where, years later, he'd wait in front of Beasley's. No shoe store then. He was six or seven. Near the spot where Beasley's would open was an Arapaho Indian trading post. Howard figured the Indians behind the counter (there were two of them) weren't really Indians, though now he wondered what made him think that. What did he know about Indians? Maybe they *were* Arapahos and he couldn't face these disconsolate men in their white shirts and khakis, forced to wait on people as silly as his mother and her sister. The women traipsed up the aisles picking through fringed leather jackets and beaded moccasins: "Girl, *this* will slim you down!" or, "No, your face looks swollen in that hat, girl, put it back!" Maybe the men weren't "authentic," but they seemed crushingly sad, stuck with all this stuff. Even a kid could see how rotten the merchandise was, rubber tomahawks and plastic headdresses with fake, dyed feathers.

One Saturday, after trying on shirts for two and a half hours, he followed the girls to the trading post—a "treat" for him after being so good in the clothing stores, his mother said. In fact, the place always depressed him. They were the ones who loved the gaudy trinkets. He desperately needed to pee, and a piece of paper taped to the men's room door said "Out of Order." The girls forced him into the ladies' to "do his little business." They said they'd stand inside the door, barring others from barging in. (Why not *outside* the door? What were they thinking? *Were* they thinking?) They'd turn their backs so he wouldn't be embarrassed. Fat chance! He stood above the toilet bowl, straining. Nothing happened. His bladder burned. "Hurry up, son," his mother said gently, her voice muffled and echoey in the tiled room. It didn't smell like a place where a man would do his business: sickly sweet, like a field of dampened flowers. His mother lighted a cigarette and offered one to his aunt. He looked up and saw on the wall, in delicate purple handwriting, the word "Fuck."

"What's 'fuck'?" he said, his own voice impossibly loud.

His mother rushed up behind him, digging her hands into his shoulders. "Howard, don't you *ever* use that word!" she said.

The surprise pressure of her fingers released the tension in his bladder, and he sprayed the room. "Howard, Howard!" his mother screamed.

"Girl, you're going to need new shoes," his aunt said.

Back on the sales floor, *his* shoes, a pair of red, high-topped Keds, squeaked and stuck to the warped brown floor. The men behind the counter watched him quietly. He looked at his feet, avoiding their eyes, pacing the aisles. What lay beneath this waxy, cracked linoleum, Howard wondered. An Indian burial ground, bones and knives and arrowheads?

● ● ● ●

The clock at the mall's far end, above the JC Penney sign, struck noon, a recorded series of chimes replicating, flatly, the sound of the courthouse bell that once stood about four blocks from here. The courthouse had a giant clock the color of vanilla cheesecake, with big, chocolate hands. It faced Main Street from a turret atop the baroque brick building trimmed with wood.

The bell swayed in a small, square belfry behind the clock. When he was twelve or thirteen, Howard saw *Vertigo* at the two-dollar moviehouse downtown, next to the Indian trading post, and afterward he could never walk past the courthouse without imagining beautiful blonde girls in terrible peril in the belfry.

Ten years ago, state officials had declared the courthouse unsafe in the event of an earthquake. It was torn down to make room for a one-story strip shopping center. County offices were moved into a steel and glass storefront next to a new Japanese restaurant. Raw fish. *Another* eastern import.

Howard rose from the bench, his right sleeve and pants spattered with water from the fountain. He folded his hands over his lap. Where were Alina and Meagan? He'd give them another half hour. He was hungry, but he didn't want to eat the prepackaged food here in the mall. He passed a bar/café called Derrick's. A cardboard oil well stood in the window gushing crepe-paper streamers—as though it were a condiment bottle neatly dispensing its contents. Cardboard men in paper hard hats stood smiling around the well.

If Dad could have made it home each night from the fields, wearing fresh shirts, would Mama have been happier, Howard wondered, less inclined to spend the family's money? If *I'd* gotten home in the evenings, dapper and clean, would Mindy have chased her flying man?

Behind the Hard Hats, couples sat at small round tables eating salads. *Ground pepper, ma'am? Vinegar? A rubber tomahawk, to slice your tomato?*

Stop it, Howard thought. Jesus, you're slipping, old fellow.

Most days, in the last six months—all right, five (four?)—he'd controlled these random bitter surges, the dregs of his sorrows with Mindy. He had rid himself of regrets. He told himself he was ready for a visit from his daughter. Alina's presence would settle him again.

But from the moment she'd stepped off the plane (losing one of her flip-flops on the exit ramp), he'd noticed Mindy in Alina's every gesture. Her plans for shopping with Meagan and Leann showed him how little space she'd left for Daddy in her brand-name boxes and bags.

His stomach growled. Maybe he *should* eat something. He glanced inside the café. At a table near the window, a man and a woman, probably in their thirties, appeared to be arguing. An Ex-Wife Lunch? The woman stared at him, her eyes on his wet pants. He turned away, feeling the burn on his face. In that brief glimpse, she had looked just like his mother that day in the trading post, and in the family's old Polaroids: squinting in the smoke from her cigarette, impatient with the world—especially with his father, out wildcatting on some old rig.

Howard saw his face reflected in a toy shop window: sullen, comic in its seriousness, superimposed over the blue, furry head of the Cookie Monster. He laughed aloud. A young mom, leaving the store, steered her little girl away from him.

It was true, wasn't it? Shuffling behind Mindy in the bargain aisles always reminded him of his mother's tedious sprees with his aunt.

And—oh hell—was *this* the toy store? It had to be. It appeared to be the only one in the mall. He walked on, past a loud group of teenage boys with purple highlights in their hair.

Another somber truth settled in Howard's gut: his resistance to bartering had hardened in adolescence, when his sister Judy, two years older than he, took him shopping with her friends. She didn't want him tagging along any more than he wanted to, but his mother insisted that she "get him out of the house, get him a shirt or two; he's a weed, an absolute weed!"

One autumn, in the early 1970s, after a revival meeting in the high school football stadium, Judy joined a Pentecostal church in town, a development that badly frightened their Methodist mother, who admitted that hell-talk "spooked" her. For the old girl, church was fellowship, arts and crafts . . . socials with other women whose husbands worked late in the oil fields.

But Judy ate hell up. One night, Howard heard her gargling marbles behind her bedroom door. Later, she told him she had been "speaking in tongues, discoursing in the holy language of the Lord."

On Saturdays, Judy and her Jesus pals looked for dresses and shoes at a used clothing store called Second Coming, out by the cemetery and the abandoned railroad station. The place had a few boys' things, mostly mothballed suits, but Howard spent most of his time there spying on Shannon and Roni, Judy's best friends. They were "good girls"; this added a pinch of glory to their tanned shoulders and muscled calves.

Once, when Roni caught him staring at her legs from behind a rack of scarves, she smiled at him knowingly (the same smile Meagan had given him a while ago) and told him, "Our bodies are God's temples. Our beauty is his praise."

"Praise the Lord," Howard mumbled, and she laughed at him—a moment as dreadful as the Arapaho Ladies' Room Incident.

He never wanted to shop with Judy and her cohort again, but his mother made him. He'd stand in the store with his eyes on the floor so he wouldn't be tempted by the good girls' flesh.

In her first year out of high school, Judy got a job at Second Coming. The long hours kept her from her friends; they drifted apart. Eventually, shopping lost its allure for her. She no longer went to church. She spent her evenings sitting, exhausted, on their mother's front porch swing, then with boys in the backseats of cars, on cheap couches in one-room rentals, and finally on the old spring bed where her daughter was born. By then, the father, a young roughneck from Midland, had migrated to Kansas. Or Nebraska. Some other wind-scoured plain.

Now Judy lived in Abilene with Howard's niece, Ava, a twelfth grader. Judy worked in a florist's shop where, she said, the customers were either "deliriously happy or devastated by grief. Nothing in-between. Makes buying simple." In the past, whenever Howard asked her what happened to God, she laughed and said, "He needs a better road crew. Left a lot of damn dead-ends."

Implicit in her bitterness was an indictment of the oil fields. Like their mother, like Mindy, she resented the late nights on rigs, the sweat and the stink, the dust and the mud, the unrelieved flatness of the bedrock. But God Almighty, Howard thought, staring at the stores—where do they think these fancy baubles come from?

He spotted Alina with Meagan and Leann, huddled together in a place called The Sleep Shop, sifting through a pile of yellow cotton nightgowns on a bargain table. Above them, the store's ceiling glistened with flat, metallic stars. The girls laughed, pressing the gowns against their bodies, patterns of candy-cane stripes on the sleeves.

They hadn't noticed him through the window, and he stood there . . . enchanted? Strangely flushed.

He turned and walked to the other end of the mall, past a statue of a pony. The pony appeared to be smiling—surely not the artist's intention. Or perhaps it was. Everything about the mall seemed designed to turn everyone into a grinning idiot, Howard thought. He came to a storefront offering "Bibles, Inspirational Calendars, Christian Gifts." Three for the price of one—Father, Son, and Holy Ghost. A poster taped to the window announced Sunday services in the Faith Complex, a megachurch (one-stop shopping) on Highway 20 by the Happy Pals Bowling Lanes and the old ARCO oil tanks.

Mindy. Naturally, *that's* what had rattled him just now: seeing Alina and her friends—kids—casually miming the sexy gestures, and remembering the old girl in a Victoria's Secret up in Dallas, on the last trip they had taken together. Trying on and modeling lingerie for Howard.

His legs went slack. He found his bench again by the fountain. Water stung his cheek. He held his hands on his lap, a gesture that felt like shame. That day in Dallas, he had been aware how far he and Mindy had come from the afternoon at Beasley's, when high heels seemed the summit of erotic life.

Had she been trying to save their marriage (their sagging sexual history) with her little nightie-show in the mall?

Sadness. Anger. What did he feel now? Humiliation, betrayal . . . but where did the betrayal lie? In Mindy? In him? The come-ons of the *New and Improved*?

That afternoon in Dallas, he had walked through the mall thinking, "Morning in America": the era's patriotic catch-phrase. The lush display windows mimicked the national gaiety. In those days, the President appeared often on television, denying American chicanery around the world.

Not that anyone cared. The malls had been full of bright, shiny

Apples, VCRs, microwave ovens. Who gave a damn about the Soviet Union, Iran, Eastern Europe, about wasting more oil than the country produced?

Stop it, Howard said to himself. Asshole, just quit.

Because, goddamnit, those weren't the worst betrayals, were they? Nor was it the loss of Main Street, the destruction of the courthouse, the control of the Permian Basin by eastern giants, not even Mindy. He thought: let's forget it, old girl.

The worst was his mother's request. Yes, surely that was it. He glanced at the toy store. "Take me out," she had ordered Howard, a near-whisper. "I want to buy something for Ava."

By then—1985? '86?—she had outlived her sister, her husband. She had thrown away her sister's unworn moccasins (at least half a dozen boxes of the silly things, tucked in a closet), her husband's sweat-and-oil-stained work shirts. And she had stopped smoking because she was dying of emphysema. "I bought one too many packs of cigarettes," she admitted.

She had come one Saturday to visit Howard in his cheap apartment east of town. This bland monstrosity—the super new Westgate Mall—had just been built. Howard had graduated from college and gotten his first menial job in Oil and Gas. He was saving to buy an engagement ring. As soon as she finished her marketing degree down in Alpine, Mindy would join him and they'd find a place together.

In the meantime, Howard's place was tiny. His mother had decided to stay the night, though she didn't live far away. These days the smallest bit of travel wore her out. There was no place for her to sleep, so she insisted he go to the mall and buy her an inflatable mattress, the kind of thing Oil Kings floated on in their backyard swimming pools. She'd put it in the bathroom, the only available space; if he needed to pee in the night, come on in, she said, it won't bother me.

Her appearance shocked him: withered and tight, like the apple dolls in the old Indian trading post. The dolls had been stacked like Auschwitz bodies in a wooden bin in the middle of the sales floor (he'd thought this even as a child, having studied holocausts—like that of the Native Americans—in school). Her bare feet were as twisted as turnips, her features pinched and soft. A bare suggestion of who she had been.

"I want to buy a doll or something for Ava," she said. "Take me to the toy store." The mattress sighed beneath her.

"Later, Mother. Rest now." He tried to touch her shoulder, lost beneath the creases of her camisole. He patted her sleeves, feeling for anything he could recognize as the woman he knew.

Her eyes glazed. She smiled and drifted, wheezing. "Remember?" she said. Howard answered, "Yes," and waited. He was used to waiting for girls.

"It was like they called your name."

"What, Mother? What called your name?"

"Things, girl." Did she think she was speaking to her sister? "All those marvelous *things* we could buy."

"Yes," Howard said. "I'll go to the mall again, Mother. This afternoon. You rest. I'll get something for Ava. From the two of us, okay?"

When he returned, she lay unconscious in the bathroom. Whatever he bought that day, hoping she'd admire it—some stupid trinket. He didn't even remember.

Yes. Best not to stir up desires, even a desire for memory, Howard thought, staring at a mannequin's faceless head.

I don't care, he thought. I don't want. Don't want. There is nothing here I want. All I ever wanted has flown away from me.

A man and a woman passed him, the couple he'd seen eating lunch—still arguing, but at least they were engaged with each other. Watching them, Howard wondered: What is it with me? What am I so angry about? Mindy's happy. Why can't I let her have that?

Leann approached his bench. She wore a white cotton sweater with a homely collar, and a hem that bunched around her waist. Her skirt was the color of mud.

"Hi," Howard said. He kept his hands in his lap.

Leann blinked rapidly. "Hi."

"Where are the girls?"

"Shopping."

"Something wrong?"

"I'm not so into fashion," said Leann. "I'm sort of . . . you know. Not made for the stuff they sell here. Like, my weight, I mean."

"I see."

"It's okay," Leann said, slumping like a forty-year-old, a young woman in a rummage-sale body.

Something caught Howard's eye: Mindy, lurching toward him. Reckless. Fast. No: Alina, without her Seattle friend.

Leann pretended to ignore her.

"Leann, I'm sorry," Alina said. "I forgot what it's like for you here."

"It's okay," Leann answered.

"Can we go somewhere else now, Daddy?"

"Where's Meagan?"

"I'll get her."

"Sure," Howard said.

"Thanks. Can I have more money later?"

Fake bells rang at the mall's far end. A child, laughing, hugged the base of a tree.

"We'll see," Howard said. "Find your friend." Just then, he

looked up and saw Meagan on the floor above them, by the escalators. A happy, attractive young lady. She waved at them and Howard waved back.

Alina reached for Leann's fuzzy sleeve. "I'm sorry," she said again. Howard glimpsed tears in his daughter's eyes. Desire leaped in his chest. Unspecific, unquenchable desire. The faceless is a lie, he thought before he *knew* it as a thought (well—isn't that the nature of desire?). "I've missed you," Alina said to her friend. "I just forgot. Will you forgive me?"

Howard stared at his daughter's pretty, made-up face—at the worry that had started to change it. What a surprise, he mused. What a delight. The sharp particularities of girls.

The Saint

On the day I became a literary critic, Suzi became a saint. Needless to say, our sex life was over. Oh, we kept at it for a while, but our abandon was never again total.

The decisive incident occurred in a priest's office, a dark brown cubicle smelling of American cheese and bologna just off the main sanctuary in the largest Catholic church in south Dallas. The year was 1975. Peter Frampton topped the charts: a pretty boy with curly blond hair. I should have known the future was bleak. (Suzi praised the singer's nasal tones on "Baby, I Love Your Way," but then, she'd already developed a saint's forgiveness.)

The priest had spent two and a half hours hearing confessions. After that, he'd delivered an afternoon sermon to a sparse group, including Suzi and me. Was he an associate priest? An assistant? How did he get saddled with this piddly office? I'm not Catholic, so I'm not privy to the pope's pecking order. The man cleared his throat and waved us into plastic orange chairs beside his desk. "So," he said. "You two want to get married?" I glanced at Suzi.

"*I'm* getting married," she said. "He's—"

"Along for the ride," I admitted. And for the first time I wondered why Billy wasn't here. Why wasn't he there last night, instead of me, when I flipped Suzi over in their bed and took her from behind?

"May God bless you," the priest said, "but I don't understand—"

Suzi explained that she and Billy were engaged to be married, but Billy had music rehearsals all afternoon, so for moral support she'd brought a "friend." I smiled at the priest. I didn't know how Billy spent his afternoons, but I didn't buy the rehearsal story. He played folk tunes, three sets of twenty songs each—Dylan, Judy Collins, Joan Baez—in the Greenfield Pub every night. By himself. The same songs, six nights a week. How much rehearsal did he need? I remembered the first night Suzi took me to hear him. I'd just met her that morning, in a Faulkner class. In the pub, we sat at a table lighted by a sputtering candle. Between songs, Billy ordered Irish coffees and drank them like water. All evening, Suzi bit her bottom lip until it bled. "Isn't he good?" she said. She touched my sleeve, lightly.

About three weeks later, Suzi and Billy called me to eat pizza with them in their small apartment, to celebrate the delivery of their bed. Above it, they'd hung a charcoal sketch of Suzi, nude, made by an art student in an advanced class for which Suzi had posed. The figure's breasts were bigger than I estimated Suzi's to be. Billy joked that the bed's iron railings were perfect for handcuffs. Suzi raised her arms, spread-eagled above her bright red hair, and I choked on my Coors. Billy watched me, laughing.

"So what is it you do?" the priest asked Suzi. "You and your fiancé? He's a musician?"

"Yes. And I'm a grad student at SMU. Working on my master's."

The good father turned to me. I said, "Me too. American literature."

"Oh. So my little homily must have seemed silly to you."

I smiled again.

"The Great White Whale," he said, blushing. "I'm not really familiar with the novel. I just used what I've heard."

"That's all right," I said.

I hadn't listened to his sermon, his homily, whatever. I'd sat in the pew, picturing Suzi bottoms-up in bed. Christ writhed in agony in a dark painting on the sanctuary's front wall. After we left the priest, Suzi told me he'd used the Great White Whale as a metaphor for the spiritual life that will elude us and drive us insane if we approach it without the proper humility.

"Forgive me," the priest had said. To me! "I shouldn't quote a book I haven't read."

This was a stronger nod to my literary prowess than any of my teachers had offered me. I decided I liked being moral support.

Two weeks earlier, as I peeled away Suzi's bikini bottom in the swimming pool at her apartment complex, I told myself not to feel guilty. At first, I was Suzi and Billy's bashful friend. The geek who spent all his time in the library. They'd invite me for pizza and beer. Then Billy started to disappear in the middle of dinner. He'd swallow a slice of garlic and pineapple, three or four Lone Stars, then . . . gone. Later on, he got to where he'd call Suzi early—from the pub, he said—and tell her to go ahead and order the food, don't wait for me, you and Tim get started. New equipment. Sound check. Sorry.

And then one evening: "I can't believe it," Suzi said to me. "I'm your first, aren't I?"

Even now (and admitting her strife with Billy), I can only explain Suzi's behavior by imagining myself as a challenge to her vanity, and this seems a partial truth, at best.

Two nights after my "awakening," as she put it, as we drifted together in the deep end of the pool (it was ten o'clock and no one was around), it occurred to me that Billy already knew I was fucking his fiancée—he'd have to be a dead man not to know—and I must have his blessing, otherwise where the hell was he?

Suzi's suit bottom floated near an intake valve. From a radio near an open window in an upper-story bedroom, Dylan sang "All along the Watchtower." The song sounded slower than I remembered it. Then faster. Was something wrong with the radio? As I gazed at Suzi's face, wondering what we'd set in motion, the song seemed to rush, drag, rush: mental distortions, tied to my fluid moods. Intake. Outflow. Panic. Joy.

As we drove from the priest's office, I said to Suzi, "Probably only about three people in the country have actually read Moby Dick." I wasn't one of them, but I resolved to know it intimately, so I could lord it over the theory bastards at liberal arts mixers. Those squirrels hadn't read a lick.

Tears dampened Suzi's silence.

"It's okay," I said. "We can read it *together*. Aloud. In bed."

Billy didn't show and she didn't want to go hear him at the pub. I don't remember ordering pizza. What I remember is Suzi crying again when she discovered Billy's blond hairs in her bathroom sink. "He *never* cleans up after he trims his beard," she said. "And he trims it *every day*!" She sobbed. I yanked some toilet paper off the roller and handed it to her. "You're very kind," she said. "And patient. Will you do something for me, Tim?"

"Sure," I said.

She told me to sit on the edge of the tub.

"Yes?" I asked.

"Just sit."

She unbuttoned her blouse and dropped it on the black-and-white tile floor. Then she slipped out of her jeans. In her bra and panties, she lathered her legs with shaving cream and, leaning over in front of me, warned me with a mock-stern look not to touch her. She moved a plastic razor up and down her calves, rinsing the instrument beneath the faucet after each stroke. Then she washed her legs in the tub and toweled herself dry. "Fetch me my boots," she said. I'd seen them in her closet—knee-length black velvet numbers—but she'd never worn them for me. She liked to tease me that some enchanted evening she'd drive me wild with them.

I brought them to her. "Sit," she said. I went to my knees by her bed. She stripped and pulled the boots up her legs then she settled back on the sheets. "Where are you?" she whispered. I leaped up, shucked my clothes, and crawled on top of her. She gazed at the ceiling. I murmured into her cheek, licked her tears. "Shh," she said. "Shh, shh." Her sainthood had begun.

I only saw Billy three times after that. Suzi rarely mentioned him. She said the two of them met the priest twice a week for lessons in "holy marriage."

"My Catholicism has been dormant these last few years," she told me one morning over coffee. "I'd forgotten how much I love the ritual of the Mass. I mean, it's kind of corny, but it's beautiful too. Comforting. The patience behind it. The precision and grace. There's not much grace in life, is there?"

"Ah! Hemingway's credo," I said. "'Grace under pressure.' That's us, eh?"

Her face stiffened, as though she endured some inner distress.

She hadn't set a date, but she busied herself with wedding plans. We didn't tryst as often as we used to. I spent my days in the school library writing research papers or reading Melville. His biographers said he died penniless. At first, America's greatest sea epic was a failure. The critics missed the boat.

At grad school parties, I could never wield *Moby Dick* skillfully enough to KO the theorists, so I stood in a corner by the food, gobbling raw cauliflower.

I lived in an efficiency apartment just off a freeway near campus. My window overlooked an oak tree in a courtyard. That spring, it rained almost every evening, cold sheets of water pasting glossy leaves to the ground, a *shushing* rush as runoff from the downpours seeped into the soil beneath the tree.

I ate off a hot plate on my floor: canned soup, pork and beans. From my turntable, Linda Ronstadt moaned, "Ooh baby baby." A woman lived next door, a beauty about my age. She never smiled at me or spoke. Past midnight, every night, I'd hear her scream at her boyfriend while he paced beneath the tree, drunk on MD 20/20, pleading to come up. I'd peek through my window and see her pressed to the balcony rail, shouting down below—"You're drunk and disgusting! Leave me alone!"—the hem of her nightie riding up her thighs. In the rainy moonlight, the backs of her knees were as white as the coils of my cooker.

One night I dreamed of tossing her over the railing, only to run down and catch her in my arms, the boyfriend just a mulch-pile at this point, a wet mess to be raked away someday. The woman cooed "Baby baby!" as I carried her back upstairs.

On Friday nights, when I'd finished studying, I'd head over to Finches, a beer and burger joint on Mockingbird Lane near the uni-

versity football stadium. The smell of fresh bread from a bakery up
the street made me feel full whether I ordered dinner or not. A friend
of mine managed Finches. His name was Gary. He had a ginger
beard, a sly smile, and a limp. He'd shovel fries until two. Then he'd
close the place, send the help home. He'd sit with me by the bar's
stone hearth reading aloud chapters from a novel he'd hacked at for
years. It wasn't very good but I enjoyed the ritual. He'd grab us a couple of lagers—ignoring the sticky plates in the kitchen—and remind
me where we'd left off in the story. His stubborn pluck and glee, his
devotion to his awful characters, warmed me more than the fire.

On a typical Friday night, a student poets' club gathered at a
corner table, got snockered, bold, and loud, and yelled at the late-
shift girls streaming in from the Dr Pepper bottling plant across the
street. The girls shed their shoes, rubbed their pinched red feet, and
told the poets to shove it. This just stirred them up. "Hey baby, let's
couplet!" one of the geniuses would shout. They tipped poorly, left
a salty, burbling mess on the table, and mocked Gary's gait. The Dr
Pepper divas were every bit as smarmy, setting their shoes on tabletops, griping about their feet.

Gary could have told them all a thing or two (though he never
did): a jungle in southern Laos, a land mine sunk in mud; it was
pure dumb luck the thing malfunctioned just as Gary stepped on it.

"*This* is what you should write about," I told him whenever he
talked about the army. Instead, his novel concerned a black girl in a
Houston ghetto: a subject he knew nothing about, but the material
was "sociologically significant," he insisted. I'd know the importance
of this, he said, if I ever got out of the library and took a look around.

So we'd sit after closing, two literary types flummoxed by the
world: he by what he'd seen, me by all I'd missed. "10, 2 & 4"
flashed the Dr Pepper sign in front of the plant. What did these

numbers mean? I imagined them as the key to a combination safe. Inside, Linda Ronstadt. Judy Collins. Or my neighbor in her nightie. Never Suzi. Never the treasure I expected. Already, my imagination had accepted Suzi as a creature apart.

One Friday evening, the yelling started early in the courtyard. "I'm coming up there, bitch!" "I'll call the cops!" the woman said.

I switched off my hot plate and looked out the window. She wore only a white dress shirt, a man's. It barely covered her butt. The backs of her knees seemed to glow. Rain lashed the tree. The boyfriend staggered and weaved. I hadn't eaten all day, and my stomach hurt. The discomfort convinced me that no matter what the future held, I would never feel nostalgic about my college days. I wouldn't miss the rain. The tree. Or the lonely boy I'd been.

But oh baby baby, the backs of her knees . . .

I was surprised to see Billy that night at Finches. He didn't see me, or pretended not to. He had his arms around a woman I didn't know. Tall, loud: Suzi's opposite.

Thin crowd. Late spring. Some seniors—those headed for the service or their fathers' corporate boardrooms—had graduated early; others stayed home prepping for exams. Gary always worried about summer. Without students around, Finches didn't do enough business to justify staying open, and he felt unsafe with so few people in the bar.

Tonight, a local high school was holding a track meet in the university stadium. The big lights came on at 7:30, and a powdery glare bore through Finches' windows. "10, 2 & 4" flashed the soft drink sign. Maybe it was my year-end mood, maybe I missed Suzi, but as I watched my fellow revelers, I assigned the sign's numbers to the faces all around me. This boy's got ten more years to live, I thought. That one, two. In four months, disease will waste this gorgeous girl leaning against the phone booth. Eventually, that loving couple will scratch each other's eyes out. In the glary light, we all (I pictured myself among the crowd, as though my consciousness hovered above the room) resembled comic actors in a silent film. Performing gaily. Long dead.

Well. Way too morose. I signaled Gary for another brew.

I looked around for Billy. A pasty-faced young man—he appeared to be about twenty—moved among tables, setting palm-sized New Testaments next to people's condiments. "What the hell is this?" a big guy yelled at him. He wore a T-shirt that said, "My Alcohol Team Has a Soccer Problem." "What are you, boy? Some kind of preacher?"

"God loves you," the young man said.

"Ooh, and I wuvey-dovey *Him*," the big guy boomed. He pinched the young man's cheek. People roared. The Pepper girls arrived to a ragged, standing salute by the poets. Billy had vanished.

The following Monday, when I got home from the library, Suzi was standing in the courtyard, her back against the oak tree. She wore jeans and a blue halter top. Her hair was limp.

"I've been waiting," she said.

"I'm sorry, I didn't know . . . had we planned . . . ?"

"No."

"It's been a while. I've missed you."

"Billy left."

I tried to look surprised.

"I want to move in with you," Suzi said.

I touched her arm. Her skin felt cold, though the day was humid and warm. "Come on up, Suze. Tell me—"

"I don't want to talk about it. I want to fuck. I want to eat and go to a movie. Then I want to move in with you."

We stared at each other, hard—as if we'd fought. "Okay," I said.

Her hair tasted of cigarette smoke (she never smoked). Crazy. My Suzi-inspired distortions. She clung to me on the carpet, in the bathtub, on the bed. We were self-conscious, awkward. Still, in my eagerness, my head rang like a roomful of phones. *Pledge break. Won't you help? Call now. Give this couple a future.* I was perfect for her, I thought. "Let's track down the priest," I said. "Let's get married." I loved her, I loved her. Shit, I loved her.

Afterward, we walked up the street for cheap Chinese. Then we went to see *Return of the Dead* at a second-run movie theater. Suzi laughed and laughed. I wouldn't let go of her hand. She got quiet about halfway through the film. The corpses kept coming.

Take her home, put on Linda Ronstadt, kiss her where her hips begin to flare, the soft, subtle flare of her hips.

When we got to the courtyard Suzi wouldn't come up. She paced around the tree. "I can't," she said.

"I thought you wanted to move in with me."

"It's wrong."

"Wrong, like . . . *wrong?* Or wrong for you and me?"

She glared at me. "Don't you understand? Don't you understand anything?"

"Suze—"

Her feet were muddy. "Don't touch me! Don't you fucking touch me!"

I spread my arms. She turned and smacked her head against the tree. "Oh my god!" she said. She screamed and sank to the ground.

"Suze . . ."

"No, no! Get away from me!"

"Suze, is Billy . . . where is Billy?" I hovered around her, stupid as a moth.

"He's left!" she said.

"I know, but . . ."

A white flutter. I looked up. There, above us, leaning against the balcony railing, wearing the man's white shirt, was my neighbor. The beauty. She didn't acknowledge me in any way. She began to unbutton the shirt. Then she turned and slipped inside her apartment.

"I think . . . I'm beyond it all," Suzi whispered.

"No," I said. What did she mean? I helped her up. The gash on her forehead seemed minor. It stopped bleeding. We walked the six or seven blocks to the Greenfield Pub. On the way, Suzi let me hold her. Then she shook off my arm. The cut opened again. By the time we reached the pub, blood smeared her left cheek. We stood in the doorway. The room went quiet. Billy was singing "Diamonds and Rust." He faltered, quit. A lifetime's worth of expressions crossed his face; I saw him as an old man. Finally, all his emotions—panic, fear, exhaustion?—merged into a slow, sad smile. "Darlin'," he said into the mike. Suzi ran to the stage. I felt naked and dumb. I couldn't blend into the crowd. As I turned to go, I caught a glance from Billy: a generous smirk? *Is* there such a look? How had the evening gone so wrong? I walked away wondering what I'd missed that could have forced a different ending.

For a week after that, it seemed as though my life had been rolled up like a newspaper, fastened with a rubber band, and tossed into the bushes, where it lay hidden, the headlines soon forgotten.

I concentrated on finals. The end of spring term meant the end of my coursework. All that remained was my thesis—something on Melville, I thought—and mailing out PhD applications.

"Melville? *There's* an original topic," said my thesis adviser. He stroked his sparse red beard. Postcards of famous American writers lined his walls. Ralph Ellison. Flannery O'Connor. Dead lions. What purpose did their work serve, finally? Sociologically, historically, spiritually? Books, drawing dust. I thought of Gary.

The old prof opened a paper packet with his teeth and sprinkled salt over a lox and bagel on his desk. I noticed a trail of salt on the floor. Thirty years of lunches in this drab office? Didn't they have janitors in this building? I had the queasy impression I was walking on the remains of mediocre students.

"You're sure about Melville?" my adviser asked me.

"I guess. I mean, I think so."

"Well. Get started. Check with me again in about six months."

It occurred to me I should get another adviser.

Gary had been right about the summer. One late Tuesday night in mid-June, when Finches was nearly empty, two Puerto Rican teenagers stuck pistols in his face and got away with four hundred dollars in cash. "In the old days I would've chased those bastards, and caught them too," he told me later. "Now—"

The incident shook him so much he quit and took a job in the school library reshelving books. In the hour or so before the library closed each night, I'd walk up and find him in the sixth-floor stacks. We'd chat and flip through the art books on his cart. Rembrandt. Caravaggio. That lovely nut job, Picasso. I'd run thesis ideas past Gary—"Ahab and the Advent of Autism in Nineteenth-Century American Novels," "Whale as Id"—but his head was still in the ghettos of Houston.

One night, on my way home from campus, I bumped into Billy. He'd waited for me around the corner from my apartment. He sat on a curb with a tattered guitar case. As I approached, he stood and weaved a little. He'd gained weight. "First of all," he slurred. "I'm only doing this for Suzi. I wouldn't have come on my own."

I didn't respond.

"I want you to forgive me," Billy said.

"What for?"

"Hell if I know. Suzi thinks we should beg your goddamn mercy." He pulled a cardboard pack from his shirt pocket and lit a cigarette. "No, really," he said. "I took advantage of you. She was too much for me, so I dumped her on you."

My surprise prompted a laugh from him. "Thought you were getting away with something, did you?"

"No," I admitted. "I figured you knew."

"Well."

"Sorry."

"Fuck it. Suzi thinks you're a shy little saint or something and we corrupted you. Seems to me we didn't fill you with anything you weren't already full of."

"When are you getting married?" I asked.

"We're not. I'm leaving town." He lifted his guitar. "Going to try my luck in Austin. I don't know what Suzi's going to do. Become a nun or something." He shook his head. "Anyway. I promised her I'd do this one last thing for her. She said I'd be glad I talked to you, someday, when I looked back on all this." He punched my arm. "I kind of doubt it, know what I mean?" He walked away.

The next afternoon, Suzi caught me asleep in the library and asked me out for a drink. She took me to a new bar in the neighborhood, a dim room with blond wooden floors and candles in golden holders on the walls. The place looked more like a church than a bar. I ordered a beer. She sipped hard cider.

"You look good," I said. In the three weeks since I'd seen her, she'd lost five pounds, I judged. A white, inch-long scar marked her forehead. Her lips were chapped.

"Forgive me," she said.

I waved my hand. "Let's not do this."

"Why not?"

"You're not getting married."

"No."

"I love you."

"Don't," she said.

I finished my beer. Ordered another.

"'The ardor aroused in men by the beauty of women can only be satisfied by God,'" Suzi said.

"What?"

"That's Valéry. You're the literary guy. You should know that."

"Okay."

"It's where I am now."

"What do you mean?"

"Since Billy and I . . . you know . . . I've been comforted by my meetings with the priest. He's helping me gain perspective."

"On—?"

"I think I knew he was a drunk," she said. "Billy. I just didn't want to see it. The musician's life—the late nights, the girls in the bar. Naturally, he'd be tempted. All that beard-trimming! What did I think?" She tongued the rim of her glass. I felt a stirring in my body, but apart from it too. Or so it seemed. "I guess I pushed him to settle before he was ready."

"Suze, do you think . . . can we figure *us* out, maybe?"

In the candlelight she appeared to be beyond exhaustion. "The thing is, Tim . . . the ardor? We all feel it, you know. But we have a choice. We can turn it toward the things of this world or we can turn it toward the essences that lie beyond us."

"I don't know what to say to that."

She smiled. I'd seen the phrase in books—*a serene smile*—but it had always seemed "literary." Abstract and meaningless. "You're passionate about the things of this world," Suzi said. "Stories, poems."

"And you."

"Not me."

"Yes, you."

She dropped her eyes.

"You're not?" I said. "Passionate?"

"I'm passionate about the church, Tim. I'd forgotten how much. When I was a kid, and my dad took me to Mass, I felt safe. It's like . . . children and bedtime stories. The familiarity, the sameness. *Belief* is the gravy on top of all that. When my dad died, I thought I'd lost . . . *everything*. I was twelve, just starting my period—*very* significant timing, you know." She laughed.

She'd never spoken of her dad. I didn't know he'd died. How could I not know something this crucial about Suzi? I studied her eyes. What had we talked about, night after night?

We chatted more about her faith. When we parted I kissed her chastely on the cheek. It hadn't been said, but this was good-bye. I didn't think I'd see her again. As I left the bar, my anger at her—it was good to put a name to it, anger, yes, *utter rage*—clashed with a suspicion that I'd let her down, somehow.

By the time I checked in with my thesis adviser, six months later, I'd switched from Melville to Hawthorne, "The Construction of Guilt in *The Scarlet Letter* and Early American

Literature." "Hm. Well. All right," my adviser said wearily. Salt covered the floor.

I'd been accepted into the English Department at the University of Texas in Austin.

Late one June afternoon I was loading boxes into a rental car. All the things I hadn't thrown away: my turntable, the hot plate. I'd mailed a deposit to an apartment complex in Austin, and made arrangements to rent the car one-way.

The air smelled of rain and the courtyard was steamy.

The beauty passed me on the balcony as I taped shut a box. She wore a light purple skirt and a pale yellow blouse. "Going far?" she said, the only words she'd spoken to me in three years. Her face was lovely beyond belief.

"I don't know," I said. This felt true.

Before I left, I patted the oak tree where Suzi had banged her head.

I stopped by the library to give Gary some books and a set of albums I no longer wanted. The sixth floor was nearly empty. He sat in an aisle over a book of El Greco prints. "I love his portraits of people," he said. "They're like funhouse mirrors. Stretchy heads. These weird, elongated hands." He held up his own hands. He flipped pages, showed me beggars and bishops. "There's something wrong with every damn one of them."

The satisfaction he took in this made me conscious of his mangled foot. Probably it bothered him more than he'd ever let on. Not just the physical pain, if he still felt pain, but the impairment of his abilities. The poets' mockery. We'd never really talked about it, and I felt, as I'd felt with Suzi in the bar, shame at the superficiality of my engagement with people. Gary turned a page: "Saint Paul and Saint Peter," in robes like wax. Layered and thick. The saints had

large, haunted eyes, melancholy frowns, fingers as lengthy as willows. The distortions gave them an air of transcendence, as though
they weren't made of matter, weren't bound by gravity, weren't stuck
in the shallowness that seemed to be everyone's lot. I wanted to
weep. To keep my composure, I asked Gary, "How's the novel?"

He shook his head. "You know. I'll never finish it," he said.

"Come on."

"No, really. But that's all right. What the hell, eh? It's good to
have a never-ending task. Keeps you—" He grinned.

"—on your toes!" we shouted and laughed together.

"I'll miss you," I said.

Gary nodded. He turned another page: *View of Toledo*. The
caption said the landscape had been painted around 1567. The
buildings looked old all right. Cavelike. Earthen. But I was sure I
glimpsed the future there. Why did I feel this so deeply? The lime-
green of the arid-seeming hills, the bruised-looking blue of the
sky . . . they were *photographic* somehow. Like satellite shots. A
river divided the scene. Sensual and austere, gleaming brilliantly
in an otherwise desertlike atmosphere. Beauty's voice swam into
my head: *Going far?* Outflow. Intake. I squeezed Gary's shoulder
and walked to the stairs.

In Austin, I wasn't tempted to go hear Billy play. Each week, I'd see
his name in the entertainment section of the newspaper, in the club
calendars. Mellow, said the listings. A nice, mellow evening.

I didn't listen to the radio. The Sex Pistols. The Clash. Rock 'n'
roll armies. Harmony had bled from the world.

My body felt deceptive: young-looking in mirrors, but out of
tune with my real, bewildered self. On campus, the sight of couples

choked me up. This is what comes from being married to the world, I thought. Wandering in the wilderness.

As my literary studies progressed, I plunged deeper into Hawthorne's murky souls. In his fiction, the future was always glued to the past. He said once that he hoped to "connect" the "legendary mists" of bygone times to the "very present that is flitting away from us." I scribbled this quote on a note card and taped it to my bedroom wall, next to a poster of *View of Toledo*.

Then a letter came from Suzi. Postmarked Houston. She hoped I'd come see her:

> I've moved in with a wonderful man and his two daughters. Until you've shared a house with children, you don't understand the passion that drives us to unite our bodies, women and men. Oh, Tim, I wish you could know this experience! Children are life's most precious joy!

She spoke of her "continuing spiritual journey" and her "babysteps toward the all-encompassing light." We corresponded by mail for six or seven months, and even talked once on the phone. Finally she wrote to say that she missed me terribly, and it was important to her to share with me the discoveries of her new life. As a P.S. she scribbled, "I shouldn't admit this, and I do try to fight it, but sometimes I think about you and I get an overwhelming desire to touch you in a naughty way."

Damn her, I thought.

With my teaching assistant's stipend, I'd bought a used Honda hatchback. It had a hole in the dash where the radio used to be. This suited me fine. On a mild October afternoon, a week before Halloween, I set out for Houston.

●●●●

I assumed that Suzi's address would lead me to the suburbs, to a nice neighborhood near several churches and strip shopping malls. Instead, I followed the map into the city through largely black neighborhoods just west of a cluster of skyscrapers. I witnessed Gary's novel spring to life, and I thought of writing him a note.

At one intersection, a boy, about fourteen, stepped into the street as cars idled at a stoplight. He gripped a white plastic jug and a flaming torch. He lifted the jug, chugged a mouthful of clear liquid, and brought the torch to his lips. He breathed out fire, a yellow plume, serpent-like. Two little girls clapped from the porch of a rowhouse on a dirt lot close to the street. The boy strolled among the cars, collecting coins for his performance. *Sociologically significant*, I thought. I handed him a quarter.

A block away, Suzi's neighborhood bordered a bodega and a commercial strip with a gun dealer, a bail bondsman, a radio repair shop, and a shoe wholesaler. Boxy houses, all alike. Children's Halloween drawings hung in windows up and down the street: bone-men, devils. A pumpkin lay smashed on a sidewalk. In the overgrown yard in front of Suzi's house sat two small bicycles with pink banana seats. Holes pocked the driveway. A dozen or so wooden shingles had fallen off the roof and were stacked beside the garage. I parked the car. Suzi met me at the door. We hugged. She looked just the way I'd remembered her. Thin. Shoulder-length, bright red hair. A tiny white scar on her forehead.

Much gushing, much laughter. She ushered me inside. The house's interior surprised me. Immaculate. Freshly painted, yellows and greens. Wicker chairs, glass-topped tables, except in one room where there was a small black-and-white TV, a purple beanbag chair, a fraying hound's-tooth couch, and two table lamps sitting on the floor, on an orange throw rug. Painted stallions galloped across the lamps' brown shades. "Dan's inner sanctum," Suzi said. "I'm not allowed. He watches TV with the girls in here. They're at the store. Back any minute."

She offered me a Dr Pepper and we sat at a wobbly kitchen table. "I'm so glad you're here," she said. Cicadas screamed in the backyard trees. Black pecans littered the part of the patio I could see through a small window. The kitchen smelled of apples. "So," Suzi said. "Tell me about yourself."

I laughed. "Well. Where to begin?" I said. "School's okay, I guess." "Yeah?"

"Yeah. Too many theorists in the department. Nobody reads anymore. I just want to examine the structures of—"

"I don't know how you do it," she said. "I couldn't stand it. I mean, there's only a finite number of stories, right? The same ones, over and over. Coming-of-age. Love stories, death stories. Anyway, I can't wait for you to meet Dan's little girls. Stephanie and Amanda. Six and four." I tried not to reveal my irritation at her dismissal of my interests. Of course, she'd heard me say this stuff before. Years ago. I sipped my soda. As she spoke I looked for signs of her affection for me. Did any survive? A trace of naughtiness? Or was that a ruse to get me here so she could show herself off, prove to me how well she'd managed, post-Billy, post-me?

She leaned close. The smell of her hair—strawberries, peaches?—dizzied me. Yes, yes: whatever else had been true of Suzi and me, the proximity of our bodies . . .

"—a former priest," she was saying. "I have a meeting with him tonight. After dinner. Shouldn't take long. I'm sorry, I didn't think to reschedule it during your visit. Maybe Dan'll let you watch TV with him and the girls, and I'll be back before you know it. Anyway, this guy, Wayne Peters is his name, he's working as a private therapist now, counseling people like me with powerful spiritual yearnings who want something more than traditional churches can offer."

"Mass doesn't do it for you anymore?"

"I'm way beyond those rituals. They were just a starting point—for which I'm grateful, don't get me wrong. Wayne and I are exploring out-of-body travel now, *direct* communion with God without the clothing of the world, so to speak. It's so exciting, Tim."

I worked to keep my smile.

The front door swung open and two ghosts flew through the house followed by a bloated version of Billy. He looked to be ten years older than Suzi and me, sunburned, paunchy. He wore a big blond beard.

"How do," he said, and squeezed my hand. His back was stiff, or his legs, a subtle hesitation in his movements. A work-related accident or a childhood illness: a hidden story. The girls dropped their Casper masks and the wrinkled sheets, smeared with dried red paint, which they'd wrapped around their bodies. "Oh my gosh! You guys! These are the *perfect* costumes!" Suzi said to them. She kissed the tops of their heads. "You're going to be so *scary*! Stephanie, Amanda. Say hello to my old friend, Tim." They were too excited to pay me any mind. They chased each other through the living room, bumping end tables, scattering magazines. "Stephanie has stinky underpants!" the little one shouted at her sister.

Dan grabbed a Bud from the fridge and busied himself at the stove. "Tacos for supper," he told me. He heated vegetable oil in a pan. Suzi said he worked for a natural gas outfit. "To the bone," she cooed, "all for the girls and me." She hugged him from behind.

"Suzi!" he said. "Damn it, be careful. This oil is hot. Hand me those tortillas."

He acknowledged me only once more, to ask if I wanted a beer. I hadn't finished my Dr Pepper, but I said, "Sure." Suzi set the table. I stood in a back corner, underneath a hanging fern. The sun was setting. No one moved to turn on any lights. I heard the TV, the girls laughing. Dan switched off the burners, said, "Bathroom, then we're good." He sauntered down the hall.

"Isn't he great?" Suzi whispered to me.

"Yes. Great."

"Solid as cement. And so passionate!"

I smiled. The resemblance to Billy? Solidity, safety (did he remind her of her dad)? The need for kids (when had *that* happened)? Rude desire *and* the Holy Ghost—how did they fit? I understood I'd never tease out the answers. Suzi remained, for me, a series of distortions.

A burnt tomato smell hung in the kitchen. Cicada-tunes rose through an open window. No screen: small green bugs rushed in. A breeze (so warm it cooled my skin) gave me goose bumps. What was I doing here? My vanity. My lascivious hopes.

Suzi lit a long green candle on the table. The girls looked at me and giggled. Dan reached for the salt and knocked over the plastic container, spilling grains on the floor. I realized he was tipsy. I tried to watch, without staring, as he sugared tea for the girls with slow, painful stirrings. Were men like him Suzi's sin? Did she chain herself to them for the exhilaration of later breaking free of the world?

And what about men like me?

Suzi told Amanda and Stephanie, "I have a meeting after dinner, so you'll have to be good girls, be sure to brush your teeth, get your pj's on, and get to bed on time, okay?"

As she spoke, Dan drifted into a deeper silence, if that was possible. A silence *within* his silence. The girls felt it too. They looked carefully at Suzi, then Dan. About ten minutes later, Stephanie said, "May we be excused?"

"Go," Dan said.

I helped him clear the table. He moved more stiffly now. "Back soon!" Suzi called from the front porch. "You girls, you be sweet little angels, okay? Tim, there's a fresh towel for you in the back bedroom. I'm glad you're here." The door closed. For a few seconds, her absence left me breathless.

Dan stoppered the sink and squeezed soap from a pink plastic bottle into the water. I hovered nearby. "Give you a hand?" I asked.

"It's a fucking waste of time to wait up for her," he said.

"Excuse me?"

"Amanda, Stephanie! Pajama time!" he yelled. Thumping and laughter, down the hall.

Dan concentrated on bubbles rising from the sink. "I'm telling you, she won't be back till well after midnight. It's the same every week."

"Oh."

"She's falling in love with him. This ex-preacher."

"Oh."

"Way she talks about him. Wayne this, Wayne that. He goes into his God routine and it turns her ass on."

"I see."

"You don't see dick. Otherwise, why are you here?"

Right. Right. You've got me there, I thought.

"She's like a tourist of the emotions. Try it all. Find the highest possible thrill."

He was angry, exhausted, drunk—and not too smart, I thought uncharitably. But he'd nailed *this* mess about as well as anyone could.

"She'll leave me soon," Dan said. He dried his hands on a stiff yellow towel. "But you—she'll probably keep you on the hook forever, calling you up, wherever you are, to come witness her newest triumph, her latest 'growth.' And you'll jump, won't you, you son of a bitch?" I thought he was going to smash me in the face, but he staggered out of the kitchen and disappeared somewhere in the back of the house.

None of what he'd said had anything to do with me. But his barely checked impulse to hit me came from the simple fact that I was here: the solid matter confronting him.

I helped myself to another beer, thinking as I popped the cap, *Don't do this, rouse yourself and get the hell out of here.* Three hours back to Austin? Three and a half? I could sleep in my own bed tonight, not much worse for wear.

Stephanie and Amanda lay on their stomachs in front of the blaring TV. They wore ankle-length cotton gowns covered with candy cane patterns. Their hair was wet. "Hi," I said. "Do you know where your dad went?"

They shook their heads. "Will you read us a story?" Amanda said.

"Well, sure. Sure." I turned the set's volume down. I placed my beer on the orange rug and flopped into the beanbag. "Can you find me a towel?" I said. "We should dry you guys' hair, okay?"

I did that. Then they squeezed into my lap, with a copy of *Will You Be My Mother?* "We like stories," Amanda said.

"I like them too."

Stephanie smelled of toothpaste and milk, Amanda of coconut lotion. The TV said, "If you don't have an oil well, get one!"

Before I'd made it a quarter of the way through the story the girls had fallen asleep. I reached over under the stallions and turned off the lamp. The beanbag sighed beneath my weight. On the television, two motorboats chased a third one up a river.

● ● ● ●

Amanda kicked in her sleep. How long had I dozed? Light from the television hurt my eyes. On the screen, an evangelist on a stage in front of a huge American flag smacked a woman on the forehead. She fell to the ground shouting, "Thank you, Jesus!" "Rise!" the preacher said.

My skin was warm where Stephanie's open mouth touched my arm. Needles pierced my legs. A stale ground beef odor tinged the air.

Gently, I lifted my wrist. My watch said 2:46. The house was quiet. I figured I'd have heard Suzi if she'd come in. Could I stand up and get the girls to bed without disturbing them too much? Did I have the starch to make it back to Austin?

"Daddy?" Amanda said.

I glanced up. Dan stood in the doorway, his hair a sweaty tangle. Bleary. Clearing his throat. He wore no shirt. Stephanie stirred. I tightened my grip on the girls. They stared at their father. His belly heaved. He straightened his back and winced. "Praise Jesus!" said a TV pilgrim. "Son of a bitch," Dan said, and took a step forward. He reached for his side, just above his belt. I realized he was cursing his pain. "Daddy?" Amanda said. We waited, the girls and I, to see where his ardor would lead him.

He rubbed his face. I stood and slid the girls from my lap. Dan didn't speak. He picked up Stephanie, I grabbed Amanda, and we carried them to their bedroom. Adhesive stars on the walls glowed palely in the room. Right away, the girls conked out again. Dan kissed them and straightened with a groan. I backed through the doorway. "Well," I said. "Thanks for the tacos."

He ran a hand through his hair as if trying to make himself presentable—a gesture as absurd as my words.

"Say good-bye to Suzi for me," I said.

Dan nodded.

On the road I looked for a late-night coffee shop. I pinched my arms to keep myself alert. I could have used a radio. Hooters, Denny's, House of Pancakes—all closed.

I'd gotten away clean. Unmarked. "Congratulations," I said to myself. Then an image came to me of Suzi's quiet house: the girls asleep beneath their phony stars, Dan drunk and snoring, sprawled half-dressed across his bed. Suzi coming home to find me gone. It was her own damn fault, I thought. Sacrificing others for the sake of her salvation. Yet she said she'd needed to see me. She'd written me for a reason. Maybe she was in trouble. Confused over Wayne and Dan. Maybe we would have spent all day talking about it. Who could stay in a house like that?

I remembered the night she'd banged her head against the tree. As she'd doubled over, bleeding, I'd looked up—looked away—to see my neighbor on the balcony.

Why think of this now?

I stopped at a flashing red traffic signal. Houston was empty. Pink and blue light poured from a shop window, illuminating a curb cluttered with paper cups and old hamburger wrappers. The light came from Portinari's Fish Emporium. White scaly skin, open staring eyes, tentacles, shells lay among plastic price tags on mounds of salted ice in the window. The light seemed bright because of the night. In fact, the hue was ruddy, the faintness of sunset and sunrise—just after, just before. A swollen silver fish, with gills like little caves, dominated the display, the "Special of the Week." I squinted to see what kind of fish it was. I couldn't make it out. The light flickered. A suggestive wink. Keep looking, keep looking, it said. You've missed it.

Closed Mondays

M el had bought a bad car from a man who'd claimed to be his father. The man had arrived at Mel's place of business, a fake Indian trading post just outside of Clovis, New Mexico, on a Friday afternoon that threatened rain. The guy drove a 1986 Honda Accord hatchback, silver with rust spots on the hood and doors, two missing hubcaps, and a hole in the dash where the radio had long since disappeared. A foreign jobbie, laughably small next to all the Hummers and 4x4s on the highways hereabouts: the perversity of the vehicle appealed to Mel's sense of the West as a radically untethered place—a hit he'd gotten from the Sam Shepard books he'd read in college and three or four films that had once made waves at Sundance. After two years or so, these movies came and languished for a week at the cut-rate theater east of town whose owner hoped to cater to the don't-tread-on-me art house types, the Becketts of the desert who'd gone to school, read history and literature, and come out skeptical of the so-called American Dream (they always said "the so-called American Dream," never just "American Dream"). Their skepticism took the exact form of the thing it repudiated—so, postmodernism *hadn't* died on 9/11, some young Lyotard from Santa Cruz or Colorado State

always argued downtown in Buck's Java Stop. You had your ranchers
with urban sensibilities, most of whose limited ranching skills led to
foreclosures and auctions of their malnourished animals within six or
seven months, your avant-garde cowboys whose pose said, "Out here,
a man's a man, but he's in touch with his inner Annie Oakley."
Trouble was, not as many of these dropping-in drop-outs managed
to make a go of it as the census forecasts had predicted ten years ago:
you either dropped in or you didn't—*that's* your American Dream,
jack; don't tell me you're a post-Freudian Marxist while you're down
at the credit union taking out a loan on your mortgage. So the
Redford mystique just wasn't cutting it here, and the theater was a
flop. Still, Mel held the indie film/*Motel Chronicles* West close to his
heart. He took twisted delight in being a "local" with a quietly ironic
"global" view. Right away, he warmed to the Honda. It was beat to
shit, which was right for this place, but its sensibly restrained thirst
for petroleum products marked it as an anomaly in the oil-fattened,
Po Mo West. The Land(s) of (Dis-)Enchantment.

The man who'd claimed to be his father had hell's own sun-
burn. He smoked hand-rolled cigarettes, one ashen disaster after
the other, and apparently never shaved, though apparently he didn't
produce much facial hair either. Mel didn't believe the guy was his
dad, though he could have been. He came from Midland and he
knew a thing or two about Mel's mom. A thing or two is all there
was to know: Grey Goose martinis, *very* dry, three olives, starting at
seven every evening. Perpetual runs in her knee-highs. What else? A
genuinely sweet old gal.

"I'll take two hundred for it," the man told Mel just before the
rain started up that Friday afternoon.

Mel looked at the car in the cloudy, dust-filled light. "Title and
registration?"

"Don't even *make* hatchbacks no more," the man muttered.

Of *course* all the paper had been tossed. "Hundred fifty," Mel said. "Shit." The man held out his hand.

Mel pulled the cash straight from his shirt pocket: two days' take at the trading post. "How you going to get where you're going now?" he asked the man.

The man locked eyes on the ground. "I'm sorry I run out on you," he said. "And I'm shamed your Mama'd passed by the time I got around to missing her." He tugged a black matchbook from the back pocket of his jeans. The cover said "Dog House Lounge, Midland, Texas." "You ever . . . you know . . . this is where you'll find me." He scribbled "Jerry K. Hibbings, Pop" inside the matchbook cover and handed it to Mel. He slapped the cash against the palm of his free hand. "You done your old man a favor here today. And I'm happy to help my boy get a few miles down the road."

Nope. That last line crossed the bounds, Mel thought. Until then, the old fellow had played it pretty well. Avoiding the saccharine, avoiding details. Gliding on the sheer boldness of the approach. Hooks, simple scams—they're never as easy as they look. You ride whatever moves. After all, Mel was a fake Indian. He could accept, even appreciate, a fake dad. *Give us this day our daily cornmeal, and forgive us our price-scalping as we forgive those who scalp us.* Oh yes, the desert was full of these folks, drifters and grifters and truckers and service station vending machine suppliers with a little black market on the side, lost souls hoping to fuck up other lost souls by the most obvious and sentimental means—methods that usually worked because even a screw-job was interesting, something to talk about over tequila at the end of another sun-numbed day.

The man pocketed the cash and started walking. It wasn't for another six hours, while he lay in bed with Wilma listening to the force of the rain whip dogwood leaves against the back of the house, that Mel was tempted to go after him. Not for the dad-stuff—or to find out how the fellow had figured him for a mark, knowing Mel would tumble to the "long-lost" bit—but because he'd realized, during the evening, without thinking much about it, what throw-aways they were, he and the other self-employed, high desert hipsters who met at the roadhouse after work to polish each other's detachment. They were children of alcoholics or addicts—straight from the loins of Loathing and Fear—and most of them were on their way to replicating the inebriated exploits of the missing and the dead. This, he had cottoned to tonight, as the radio warned of flash flooding and he pictured the man walking down the road, away from the trading post, was the *real* reason they'd dropped out in the middle of the wasteland, pretending to long for stability (whatever the hell *that* is, some drunken Baudrillard would shout).

The desert-huddle didn't cradle him, didn't distract him from his debts anymore. Besides—something *interesting* had happened to him this afternoon! He'd purchased a junker from a stranger who'd shown up out of the blue, out of the summer's first dirty blue thunderheads (and the shadows they cast on the land), a codger with an outlandish story that had as much chance of being true as a douser's willow stick, and they'd played it casual with each other, like they both had something to lose if the transaction hadn't reached a satisfactory conclusion.

He left Wilma asleep in the bed and walked to the dark kitchen for a glass of tap water. Rain licked the window hard, now soft the way Wilma used to run her tongue up and down his chest. He laughed at himself for imagining this. Things were finished with Wilma, just as they were over with the trading post. He'd been aware of these seismic shifts for eight or nine months now: the last time it *really* rained. Funny, how heavy the sun could sit on your skin. And the moon. Hot and cold, gripping you tight.

Wilma knew this parting would come. Mel felt sure of that. She had once been married to a member of the Oklahoma House of Representatives who, when he ran for the U.S. Senate, decided (maybe rightly, maybe wrongly—who could predict the American electorate?) that her Kiowa blood would be a career-killer. Wilma was a creature who could scissor-kick her way through any damn flood.

Mel spent the rest of the night watching her sleep, the curve of her back like the curve of a scallop shell: an object, a shape you couldn't find for hundreds of miles in any direction on this parched plain. He knew what he was leaving. But something interesting had happened this afternoon, and it made him acknowledge that nothing much had happened to him in a long time. The false, knowing apathy that was the currency of his compatriots had become real and flinty and killing. He couldn't fake it anymore: fake indifference, fake horniness. *Fake Indian* (that had been Wilma's idea, not a bad one, just another idea in a world full of the fool things, canceling each other out). The falseness had hardened on him, and he'd have to pay for letting that happen—how had he let that old man walk away?—by shedding the externals, finding his soft skin again and admitting he was just an infant, ready to bawl his guts out.

Buck's Java Stop opened at dawn and Mel was there for a tall one, Guatemalan, Room for Cream. The place was tricked up like a Starbucks, with abstract but vaguely happy sun-faces painted on the menu board, green tabletops and chairs. Buck sold the *New York Times* (always two days late because of delivery problems) and music CDs (local artists, mostly), but from the look of things, the merchandise wasn't moving. Buck needed a fresh gimmick. An old poster for the cheap-seat theater hung, torn and curling, by the door.

At an ARCO station on the east side of Clovis, Mel filled the
Honda's tank. Less than twenty bucks! Perverse. Moderation in Oil
Country, in the Republic of Natural Gas? It wasn't right! ARCO
didn't even exist anymore. Mel had read this in an old edition of
the *Times*. British Petroleum had bought the company out. West is
east. Po Mo, man. Shifting sands.

Yesterday's rain was just a rumor now. The desert had regained
its crusty surface. More than once, as he headed for the Texas state
line, tattooed men in semis crowded Mel, like they wanted to run
him off the road. What was this hatchbacked rust-bucket doing on
the good and true path?

He shook his head. He still saw things with a cynic's hard brain.
But what was he feeling? Yes, what *was* that, stirring in his belly?
"Buck's coffee," he said aloud. "That's all." Then he called himself a
shallow, sodden prick. He was practicing, practicing finding the
pained, soft skin.

The car sputtered and chugged. The clutch was hit and miss. It
wasn't until he'd reached southeast Midland—rows and rows of refinery tanks and an electrical power station—that it dawned on Mel: the
old man couldn't have walked here by now. Not that he'd remained on
foot, necessarily. Or headed back here. Why would he turn around
and make *himself* a mark, a target for those he'd wronged?

Mel looked at his face in the rearview. "What are *you* after?" he
asked his reflection.

He found the address on the matchbook cover, stopped and
asked directions at a 7-Eleven. The lounge turned out to be a boxy
cinder-block building, painted pink, squeezed between two billboards: "Country the Way Country Should Sound" and "Pregnant?
Call—" The lounge had no sign, only, in black paint on the front
wall, DOG HOUSE, CLOSED MONDAYS.

The car didn't want to die when Mel turned the key and pulled it out of the ignition. It choked and rattled a few times, then sighed and gave up the ghost. Mel felt pretty sure it wouldn't start again, but he didn't want to know. He got out, stretched, listened to the sound of gravel under his boots, and shut the door. The air smelled of refineries, tortillas from a nearby café. The sky was a faded, no-rain purple, illuminated now and then by flash-lightning.

The Dog House was every lounge that Mel had ever entered. At the end of the bar sat his mother. Not his mother, of course, but it might as well have been her. Straight scotch, no rocks, instead of a three-olive martini. If she'd worn hose, the runs would have resembled interstates on an out-of-register service station map. As it was, her varicose veins did the trick.

On the far wall, behind an unused stage, a Dallas Cowboys cheerleaders poster, at least ten years old. Guy Clark on the box.

An avuncular man sat at a table, a "Mama's friend" character, the kind that had fattened "Mama's little kitty" over the years, which along with his athletic scholarship had helped Mel get to college.

Behind the bar, a pasty man with a big head hunched over a wet blue rag. Mel opened the matchbook in front of the man's face. "Seen him?" he said. If nothing else, he figured, he'd learn something about the fellow who'd ditched the car until the fellow turned up. *If* he turned up.

"Jerry Hibbings?" the bartender said. He squinted at Mel in the dim blue light that came from somewhere above and to the right of the bar. "Jerry Hibbings died. Long time ago. Three, four years."

Mel blinked a few times, lowered the matchbook to the bar. He ordered a beer to cover whatever he was feeling. Well, hell. Fake Indians, fake faked fathers.

Almost certainly, the Honda was stolen. But he'd known that.

All along, he'd known that the most interesting thing that had happened to him was the car itself, the precarious question of how far it would take him before it conked out or got him in trouble, or both.

He turned to his mother. She nodded, half-asleep over her scotch. He thought of Wilma in their bed—her bed—waking up without him. Always in the mornings, before their anger flared, before either of them had come fully awake, she'd reach for him under the covers just for the warmth of his body. The only real moments he knew.

Like this. This is what I came for, he thought, watching the woman shake herself awake. He also thought: all my life I've been weeping, without sound and without tears. She smiled at him. Then her attention drifted to a silver television set on a shelf behind the bar. The screen was blank. "Now, *that's* some scary shit," she said. "Look at that."

Mel left his beer untouched. He dropped some change on the bar. Without thinking about it, he crossed out the word "Pop" on the inside of the matchbook cover, said, "Here you go, honey," and slid the matchbook next to the woman's drink and a soggy yellow napkin. "Jerry K. Hibbings. Just ask for me. I'll be around. I'll take care of anything you need."

"Thank you, sweetie," she said. She gave him the warmest smile.

He turned and left the lounge. In the gravel parking lot he opened the car door and left the key inside. A half-moon poked up, low in the west. Little tongues of flame rose from the intricate tubing and steel pipes of the refinery across the road, whose sign said, without irony, "Working hard, to bring you a Golden Tomorrow." Mel walked.

The Leaper

G riffin stopped the car on the eastern side of the bridge, near a concrete pylon black with old algae. All around the bridge, the land, crusted and mildly hilly, seemed haunted by the absence of water. Could wood and steel confess dispiritedness, Griffin wondered. The bridge appeared to be ashamed of its presence here. Splinters and rust; shadows of vines and vanished plants imprinted in the textures of the wood; the skin of the steel, rough-hewn and flaking.

The bridge had always been a mistake: built to the wrong specifications. Its pitch was too steep, causing dizziness, drivers claimed. And it swayed. Concrete, steel, and wood were not supposed to *sway*, swore Griffin's mom when he was just a boy, so she always left the car, politely but firmly, whenever Griffin's father, driving the family out of town for a picnic or a visit to nearby relatives, approached the bridge. "Ain't gonna see Glory at this rate," Griffin's dad called to her as she slipped from the front seat. She'd grip the bridge's railing and mince forward in her fine leather heels (which she always wore, even for an outing in the wilderness). "If I get there, I'll get there *alive!*" she yelled in return.

Early on, Earl, Griffin's brother, two years older, joined her in her stilted walks across the bridge, while Griffin and his father drove its length, parked the car, and waited for them on the other side. "We coulda made it as far as Mexico City by now—coulda been sipping margaritas—if you hadn't held us up," said Griffin's father, arms crossed and sweating on his chest.

"Don't you nettle me, old man, else I'll throw myself off this infernal contraption and then you'll be sorry," said Griffin's mother.

Her husband told her, "It's like the two of you don't *want* to leave town."

The family's bedrock truth. Griffin's mother never ventured more than a few miles from the place; she died while Griffin was finishing college, up in Dallas. Earl dropped out of high school when he was seventeen and went to work in the Eagle Valley Paper and Box Factory, the only job he would ever have.

Now, nearly thirty years later, Griffin had returned to Texas for his brother's funeral. Years ago, he'd heard that the river had dried up—where does so much water go?—but to see the sandy bluffs emptied of moist vegetation, to hear the heightened *zizzle* of the horseflies (no longer muffled by the rapids), to smell the bready staleness of sun-touched stones stiffened Griffin's spine and made him feel old.

A sign next to the pylon said he'd face a thousand-dollar fine if he drove across the bridge. It was closed now. These days, the way into town lay six miles south of here, on a brand-new bridge near the railroad trestle.

He could get back, but not the way he used to. Or the way he used to *be*.

He recalled how, on weekends, people paddled wooden canoes down this stretch of the river—children, families. People rode horses along the banks.

A metallic ticking rose from the idle engine beneath the rental car's hood. The drive from the El Paso airport (the nearest, though it was more than a hundred miles away) had been arduous. He'd forgotten what it was like, driving in the Lone Star State: the chalky dust, the harsh southern light, the challenge of desert roads, often ill-paved. How did the old joke go? *Crossing Texas ain't a trip. It's a career.*

Griffin squinted against the four o'clock light, across the bridge and the gulch where the river had once coursed with so much care-less power toward the Bottoms, the lip of town where the poorest factory workers used to live—probably still did. Griffin didn't know. He'd lost touch with his brother through the years.

"*Professor*," Earl used to drawl into the phone, back in the days when they still called each other on holidays and birthdays. Ten, fifteen years ago now? After school, Griffin had moved out west to teach in a small liberal arts college on the Oregon coast and to write books on the pastoral tradition in twentieth-century Irish poetry.

"Brother," Griffin answered Earl, on the phone.

Inevitably, their conversations turned to Griffin's betrayals—a word Earl never used (like many West Texas men, he rarely used words at all, and would have been happy, Griffin thought, as a mute), but it suffused the very timbre of his voice. Griffin had "gone and got educated" (betrayal number one), left Texas (two), and devoted his imagination to some misty, far-off place (case closed).

Like the bridge, he'd been badly engineered.

"Ireland's in our blood," Griffin tried to argue with his brother. "Our ancestors come from there."

"Who *all died* hundreds of years ago," Earl countered. "You're a *Texan*. What the hell does Ireland matter to us?"

Truth be told, Griffin wasn't sure he knew the answer to this

question, beyond his passion for Irish rhyme and story, which he'd
first heard in high school right here in Eagle Valley, Texas—an
eccentric English teacher hated by all the other kids (what had happened to *her*? Evaporated like the river, he supposed; like his
mother; like a whole generation in town).

Besides, the Irish, historically oppressed, knew enough not to
trust their deepest feelings—a relief to Griffin, for Texas demanded
of its children firm allegiance to nation, state, family, church, and
place—above all, place.

Never leave. That was the message in public prayers, pledges to
the flag, football fight songs. And if you did: betrayal.

"You care more for some old Irish blatherer than you do for
Mama, Daddy, and me," Earl accused him regularly.

"Of course not," Griffin said. But listen, he wanted to add, listen to a wise old blatherer, your distant countryman, a poet named
Seamus Heaney: "the actual soil / . . . doesn't matter; the main
thing is / An inner restitution."

What does he mean? Listen: he's treading carefully (like Mama
on the bridge), *mistrusting the ground beneath his feet*. The Long-
Term is a lie, Big Brother. Nation, State, Glory. The river. The Irish
know—the *poets* know—you're damn lucky if you can see the next
step ahead of you.

"Yeah, well, just think about it, bro. What is it *I* do?" Earl challenged Griffin one night. Beneath his voice on the line, Griffin
heard the hiss of long-distance emptiness. "I make paper so you can
have something to scribble your goddamn wisdom on. Where
would you be if I hadn't stayed put, huh?"

Brother, where does this bitterness come from? Griffin longed
to ask. But he had to own up to the fact that probably he'd already
grasped the answer.

● ● ● ●

There were betrayals, and then there were betrayals. He sat quietly beside his rental car. His first treason wasn't his embrace of poetry and the Emerald Isle. This much was certain. It was a small wooden bench in the Bottoms, near the paper plant. In the shadow of the bridge.

One night, Griffin's junior year in high school, he sat on the bench with Martha Henshaw, who, like Earl, had dropped out of school to work in the factory. Martha had just gotten off shift, and Griffin had skipped supper with his family to meet her.

They didn't speak. Her fingers brushed his lips. He turned soft as smoke inside. Clouds scattered over the river. Her hand opened on his chest. Together, dizzy above the water (water sipping clay, spinning leaves, drumming stone) they lifted like divers off a high board in a gold and sudden flutter.

"Griffin!"

The tug back down.

"Griffin, what the hell are you doing?" His brother's voice. Night. The bridge. The moon going green, behind the factory's processed clouds.

"Leave! Now!" Martha whispered to Griffin. He saw it in her eyes: she wished to rush onto the bridge and leap into the river. Instead, she turned to face Earl—her lover of nearly a year. Griffin, the pesky younger brother who'd never let the couple be, who from the first had quietly flirted with the girl, scrambled down the riverbank.

Leave. Yes. And so Griffin had, by slow degrees—all the way to an imaginary Ireland. Bitterness? Well. But he and Earl had managed through the years. It's true they'd never trust each other again, not quite. They'd engage in heavy sparring on the phone. But at least they'd stayed in touch. And even when the phone calls stopped, it wasn't the sign of a rupture. Their father had died. Peacefully, in his sleep. Griffin had returned to Eagle Valley, briefly, for the funeral, eaten a meal with Earl and his wife, and after that, for the next ten or fifteen years, there simply wasn't a compelling reason for the two of them to talk. Earl sank into his natural muteness, and Griffin accepted that. No hard feelings, just . . . no feelings at all.

Martha? Long forgotten. Earl had married someone else and stayed married, apparently happily, for over twenty years. Griffin, who had left for college a year after the night on the bench, didn't even know what had happened to the lovely Miss Henshaw.

Lost water. Under the bridge.

Then last month, the call from Earl's wife, a quiet woman named Lori. The lung cancer, she whispered. An unexpected return. This time it was brutal and swift.

Squinting now in the afternoon light at the green haze beyond the bridge—a *reeking* haze, an odor like a bee sting, if stings left a residue, acrid, sharp, the smell of paper being made—Griffin wondered just how unexpected the illness was, if *this* was the air you breathed.

Even the river couldn't survive it.

He heard a soft slapping of hooves, and turned around: a young woman on a peanut-colored pony, galloping up what used to be the riverbank. She wore a dazzling white shirt. Griffin caught only a glimpse of her before she disappeared over a squat, craggy rise.

A strange music swelled above him in the girders of the bridge: a humming shriek of steel in a burst of wind, a knocking of wood, like an old man cleaning his pipe on a tabletop (one of Griffin's fondest memories was of watching such a man in a Derry pub one night, on his first and only trip to the north of Ireland five years ago. All evening, the man had told him ghost stories of people lost on the moors, in the bogs).

A grand and rolling wail from deep inside the bridge, the nails and bolts, as if the whole structure wanted to rise and slink away, having outlived its usefulness.

The actual soil doesn't matter. The main thing is an inner restitution.

Shading his eyes, scanning the uppermost reaches of the steel frame, Griffin registered another white flash, this time on the bridge. Was the girl on the horse crossing the gulch? No. He lowered his gaze to pinpoint the movement. Too late. Whatever it was vanished over the bridge's far side.

He swore in just the glimpse he'd had it appeared to be (naked? did that account for the startling whiteness?) a person leaping into the sun-baked river-trace.

Griffin scrambled up a dusty bluff next to the pylon. Gingerly, he placed a foot on the bridge's sloping surface. The girders sang. He clung to the cable railing, the way his mother used to do while his father waited in the car. He made his way to the center of the structure where the figure he thought he had witnessed had jumped. He peered over the side. If a body had plunged into the packed sand below—an arrow piercing flesh, a knife falling from the sky (yes, by God, he knew his Irish poets!)—it would have left a small crater, not to say a rather gruesome corpse.

Nothing. The bridge swayed. Griffin's head spun. He sat against the singing steel, and felt the song in his bones.

All right, he consoled himself. This isn't so strange. Traces of memory, of *false* memories (the leap his mother never made to spite his father; Martha Henshaw's almost-hurtle into the river). The smoke of guilt? Absences. Hauntings. The vast desire for movement, *any* movement here, now that the water was missing.

He stood, steadied himself with the railing. All still, below. Open and empty. Gravel, rocks. Heat-gorged weeds.

In the moaning of wind in the steel, he caught an echo of Lori's voice as he had heard it two days ago on the phone. "I'll box up a few of Earl's things for you," she had told Griffin, audibly swallowing tears. "You can take them with you after the funeral."

"No no," he'd said. "There's nothing I want."

"I know his stuff ain't worth much—"

"That's not it."

"—and you ain't got any use, at home, for silly trinkets from Texas—"

"Lori, I just don't want to trouble you, that's all."

"Griffin. Sometimes some of us *like* to be troubled, you know? In spite of what it looks like."

It was as though she'd bit his lower lip. Immediately, and ever since, he had swallowed Lori's words, carried them in his body— they had *cost* this quiet woman, he knew, just as the meaning behind them, as far as he could make it out, may have cost his brother, and they served as the final indictment of Griffin's betrayals over the years. A mute howling that would never cease, as lacerating as the wind on Shannon's waves.

Still, what would he do with a box of his brother's things? He looked up. Of course, he thought, shading his eyes against the sun. The white flash, the leaping figure: it wasn't a memory at all, nor a wistful haunting, a guilt-induced fantasy. The sun, burning itself up, made everything clear to him now. An illusion, but . . .

The future. That's what he'd seen. Surely, that's what the straining was all about in the flexing of the girders. The music he heard was the music of matter wrenching toward its end.

He would take the box and throw it off the bridge, at last freeing his brother from this god-awful place. *In spite of what it looks like.* He envied me, Griffin thought. Did he envy me? The phone calls, not bitterness and hate, but jealousy—and not just Martha, long ago. Nothing as small as that. What was it he'd said? "Where would you be if I hadn't stayed put?" How had Griffin missed the longing in those words? Surely his brother wished to cross the bridge. Why he hadn't done so, Griffin would never know.

It's the least I can give him now, he thought.

Just as he, in some way, kept me *here.*

Griffin glanced at his watch. He still had two hours before motel check-in and the call to Lori. The funeral was tomorrow morning. Tonight, there would be a small supper with Earl's old friends, none of whom Griffin knew. Afterward, maybe, Lori would give him the box. Would he bother to look inside? He figured he wouldn't.

He stepped carefully off the bridge and down the embankment beneath it, past brittle old rattlesnake skins, translucent as fingernails, scattered bird's nests, tiny animal bones whose peaceful arrangement in the sand belied the violence that must have left them there. *The actual doesn't matter.* His eyes prickled with sweat, with the factory's foul air. He walked to the place where the leaper would have landed. Here, according to his vision, the box, his brother's leavings, would land. Griffin stood there in the river's past track, on a small incline that cradled the future. He gazed up at the bridge's faded arms and tried to see the next few hours of his life.

The Republic of Texas

It's a mistake when water collects out here. Rain, mist, dew—the instant moisture hits the ground, the land burns it up because water doesn't have a place in the desert's natural march, which is ever and always toward obscurity and filth. I'm not speaking ecologically. I'm talking about the soul.

It's the summer they killed Timothy McVeigh. I have an interest in this because Timothy McVeigh killed three of my friends when he blew up the Murrah Building in Oklahoma City. I was living in the city at the time, working as a bank clerk. Shortly after my friends' funerals (in one instance, we buried only an arm and a leg), I quit the job and left town.

The thing is, I used to see these hoodlums—kids fourteen, fifteen—milling around Fifth and Robinson after dusk, once the crowds bearing garlands for the rescue workers had gone. The boys would get as close as they could to the chain-link fence draped with teddy bears and rain-smeared notes to the dead. They'd point at the void where the building once stood and smirk and spit and laugh. Hoodlums? More like little Nazis, with shaved, pointy heads.

Once, I confronted two of them. I used to stroll near the Survivor Tree at night, staring at the absent building, the moonlit emptiness, the glass shards, fine as webbing, seared into the ground. "What the hell are you laughing at?" I asked the boys. It was a Wednesday evening in May, unseasonably chilly. The boys were lean, and they appeared to be frightened. They looked at me, looked at each other, and spat on the sidewalk. Simultaneously. A choreography of adolescent spite. Then one of them punched me in the kidney and they ran. As I doubled over in shock, I felt nothing. I swear, not a thing. A week later, I said good-bye to my remaining friends. I drove to the old cemetery south of town with its inexpensive lots, said "So long" to my parents' graves, and left OK City.

Now I move across dry earth, in the early morning or at dusk. My thoughts spin into fragments.

Mama wouldn't put up with me. Not like this. She was a teacher. Words were her job. "Listen, Richard, a good metaphor can dissolve any knot," she'd tell me. Honest to God. That's how she talked. She'd say, "With words, Richard, you can make sense of the most perplexing things."

With scattered words now I try to call her back . . . as well as my brother and me. A sweltering afternoon. Bo and I sitting in the backseat of my parents' car, riding through the plains of Oklahoma. Where were we going? To a job interview, probably, another meeting for Papa with an oil man or a rancher. Papa driving. Silent as ever, except to demand from Mama the Jameson's from his flask in the glove compartment, or to curse the "wetbacks" for destroying the nation, crossing the Rio Grande to take jobs from hardworking Americans. "I mean, look around you, June. They've turned this country into a tidy little hell," he'd say.

Bo and I dripped sweat. The palms of our hands stuck to the plastic seat covering. These trips, with our father fuming or quiet, always frightened us a little.

Mama wrapped ice chips from a thermos in our daddy's handkerchief, leaned over the back of the front seat, and held the handkerchief against each of our foreheads. First Bo, then me. I stuck out my tongue to catch the leaking icemelt. The drops watered the words inside me, bringing them to life: a good metaphor. Mama would like it, I thought (after all, it was a variation of things she often said). I'd open my mouth and speak.

I've always thought Bo married her, years later. He wanted Mama in a woman. So did I, but I figured no woman would have me. Too much Papa in my bones.

At Bo's wedding reception, six years ago in Oklahoma City, my brother stared at his bright new bride across the room and assured me, as we lifted our glasses to toast the years ahead, "This, little brother, is a joy beyond words."

Say nothing? Or say it all?

To whom can my words matter now?

Well, here they are, the whole damn story: one miscarriage, our mother's death from leukemia, a couple of lost jobs, and Bo's joy had blown away. It seemed to me, watching him, that getting older, walking out of the house and into the world, was like climbing a staircase in the dark, in the open air—which step would be your last?

He was four years my senior. Whatever claimed him now would come my way soon enough. I kept my finger to the wind.

Nothing we said could ease our pain after Mama left us—which didn't keep Papa from talking. "Pay and pay," he slurred between liquored bouts of silence. "Believe me, all your lousy lives . . ."

"You old boot. What the hell are you chattering about?" I challenged him one night on the front lawn, while the sky threatened rain and Mama's garden, neglected since her death, hung in brittle ribbons all around us. Twigs. Yellow leaves. "Pay for what?"

He laughed at me and went inside to pour another whiskey.

"What the hell are you laughing at?" I shouted at the slamming screen door.

Soon after that, Bo and his wife, Jenny, fled the city—to escape their "misfortunes," Jenny said (Bo liked it that she spoke so much like Mama). I had no one to talk to until I went to work at the bank.

Then one day the wind changed. Timothy McVeigh slipped into the city in his dirty yellow Ryder truck.

Out here in the evenings, miles from town, you can't hear anyone. But you can smell people. It's the wind. It brings them close. Even though you're alone, you think someone might start talking to you. No one ever does. So you try to say something, just to keep yourself company, but your parched throat sticks to itself and the words won't come. You stand planted, longing for a thunderstorm, just a brief one, to cool things down, to loosen all the talk trapped inside you.

● ● ● ●

"You like that, huh?" My father weaving above me, his puny fists in my face. "Talk to me, boy. You want me to hit you again?"

Ever since I could remember, he'd threatened to smack Bo and me, to make us pay for our mistakes, our immaturity, our laziness. "Lazy boys like you, wasting all your time . . . you'll be the ruination of this nation," he'd say. "It's 'cause of *you* the goddamn wetbacks think they can sneak in here and soak up all our jobs." He'd never actually raised a hand to me until the day we buried Mama. I was twenty-two. He was frail. The funeral had ended early in the afternoon. Afterward, neighbors brought food to the house. Mostly, that day, Papa behaved. He didn't really know these people, and they didn't like him—they were Mama's friends. They looked after him on *her* account.

They offered condolences. He'd bristle: "Hell, she was *happy*! Would have been happier if it wasn't for the damn illegals, keeping men like me off the payrolls. Up to me, I'da gotten her *out* of that school, away from teaching."

Now the house was empty. Just Bo and me and Dad. On the dining room table, platters of half-eaten chicken, casseroles, salads. Papa was drunk. He was hurting, he was angry, and someone had to pay, so he hauled off and hit me. "You think she wasn't happy? Is that what you think?" he said. "I see it! Right there on your face!" Physically, I didn't feel a thing, but I fell back into Mama's old rocker as Papa loomed over me. I couldn't defend myself or attack him in turn: he'd be dead too, within a month or so. That was pretty clear. Without Mama to steady him, booze and lack of character were going to finish him. So I sat in the chair, trying not to laugh at him, trying not to cry. "You like that, huh?" he said. "Want some more?"

Bo moved through the dining room with a white plastic spoon, scooping leftover potato salad into Mama's Tupperware containers.

Then, a few months after Papa died, along comes another son of a bitch. Timothy fucking McVeigh. Someone owes me the good life. Someone's got to pay.

"Just say it," Mama said.

I stammered, "I don't . . . I'm . . ."

"Richard, just say it!" she urged me. Pushing, always gently. "Whatever's on your mind. Don't fret about mistakes."

She taught high school English: what choice did I have but to honor words? Or at least to pay attention. "Isn't it amazing?" she'd ask whenever she wanted to boost my confidence or get me to assert myself. In those moments, usually on the porch swing, sitting in the shade of the house overlooking the front lawn and her garden, I knew she was about to launch into one of her school lectures. Her airy talk, far removed—as far as I could see—from things as they were. But her speech was always pretty to hear. "Your body's at the mercy of time," she said. "Yet your body carries language *within* it: a timeless seed of meaning. Richard! Language," Mama would say, tapping the top of my head. "It's the outward manifestation of your innermost being."

(All around us—east, west—the plains of Oklahoma. Filthy. Obscure. But the lawn and Mama's garden were straight out of the movies: perfect, unchanging, small-town America. Nothing can hurt me here, I thought.)

I'd stare at her, flummoxed, more wordless than ever. Wind. Open space. A vast, flat mistake. Somewhere out there, my old man stumbled around, wasting his days. Often, he'd stay gone a week or more. Then he'd come home without an explanation.

"Richard," Mama said. "Language is how the soul gets known."

When he *did* talk . . . why did he talk to us at all? "Punish" was Daddy's favorite word. "Pay and pay," he'd say.

Oh yes.

Then: "Why don't you?" Bo, last month on the phone. "Get your ass down here and house-sit for Jenny and me while we're gone."

"I don't know. I'm . . ."

"Something to do," Bo said. "Time to think. You could use it, little brother. We've fixed the place up since you saw it last. It'll be quiet. Peaceful."

He'd worried about me ever since Murrah, he said. He knew what it was like to need a new start.

"Okay," I said. "Give me a day or two."

Six years, he's lived in Marfa, in far West Texas. He works for a tax firm. In the last half decade he's risen in the hierarchy. Senior VP. This summer, his initiative has earned Jenny and him a ten-day, all-expenses-paid vacation in Europe. Who ever thought he'd get a chance to ride the clouds?

After his phone call, I closed up my apartment in Dallas, where I'd moved to tackle temp work in a mortgage firm, and drove on down to the desert. I helped Bo pack, then he and Jenny fastened little Canadian flag pins to their shirts so the bad guys won't take them for Uncle Sam's children. They waved good-bye. My brother is always waving good-bye.

● ● ● ●

This morning I get up late, shower, put on a T-shirt and my jeans. I switch on the bedside radio. My sister-in-law ("I swear, Bo, look at you—I'll be damned if you didn't marry Mama!") is also a high school English teacher. The bedroom is full of books. I pull a crack-spined Dante off the shelf. Some of the pages flake. A note in the back of the book, in Jenny's delicate hand, says that Dante was a fierce old bird, fighting to get into paradise.

On one shelf, near the bathroom, there's a framed snapshot of Bo and me as kids, in a Western-themed amusement park. We're dressed in dark shorts, black-and-white Oxfords. Laughing like crazy. Typical 1950s geeks. All that's missing are the Davy Crockett coonskin caps. Behind us, a gunslinger (a teenager in a too-big costume) mugs at the camera next to a very pale Indian. The Indian, grinning, grips a rubber tomahawk. Taped to the back of the picture frame, a piece of paper carries the legend "June 14, 1957." This is crossed out and replaced with "Jan. '58??"

Mama's handwriting. She must have taken the picture.

Then her body grew frail.

Then she left us for the wind. My father, the taciturn one, the aimless one, the one without friends, followed her two months later, as though her energy, her interests—her words—were the only things that had tied him to the planet.

For the third time this morning, a radio newswoman repeats that Timothy McVeigh died last week with his eyes open. "Witnesses on-site said he looked stoic, calm, resolute," the newscaster says. "Many of the bombing survivors and victims watching the closed-circuit feed in Oklahoma City said he looked defiant. Hate-filled. Evil."

Already this morning, the sun is out of control. Out here, on a day like today, the lightest trace of moisture sprinkles hope along your arms, on the back of your neck: like nothing, not even the passage of time, will matter if the rain comes.

Before I reach town, I smell it: the energy, the *waste* from living bodies.

Anymore, I don't know what to say to anyone.

As I enter the outskirts, a U.S. Border Patrol truck—massive, olive-green—passes through Marfa. The street is quiet, but the truck stops abruptly and two men in bulky camo clothes, wearing steel helmets and wielding big leather sticks, leap out and tear down an alley by a Savings and Loan that appears to have been closed for years. The men shout at someone I don't see.

I walk down the street, find some shade, and sit against a building. I've brought Dante with me: a mild weight to keep me anchored. A pretty young woman walks by and I follow her with my eyes. Even in the shade the light is too bright for reading. The book's pages blaze like desert stones. I get up, dust off my pants, and step into Carmen's Café, across the street. This is how I waste my days.

I'm as silent now as my father used to be.

The place is cool and dark inside—metal fan blades whirr beneath the tin-plated ceiling. A woman in a white, diaphanous scarf smiles at me from a wall calendar. The calendar is open to October 1994. Ninety-four: the year Mama died. Above the calendar, a movie

poster: *Giant*, featuring Liz Taylor and James Dean. Jerry Jeff Walker
growls from the speakers of a squatty jukebox by the ladies' room.
Three thin men share a booth whose plastic seats have ripped.
Otherwise, the café is empty.

I order lemonade, lay Dante aside. The spine cracks further and
the pages scatter. A paper placemat on the table says Marfa was
named for a minor character in *The Brothers Karamazov*, which a
visitor to this part of Texas was reading at the time. The landscape
reminded her of Russia, in another century: all the people she had
lost and left behind. The jukebox falls silent. The men talk loudly.
Gradually, I become aware of their conversation.

Two of them are trying to convince the third that Texas is an inde-
pendent nation, that a legal technicality in an 1845 annexation docu-
ment means that Texas never really joined the Union. "We're U.S.
prisoners," one fellow says, "forced to pay taxes against our wills."

The thing to do, this fellow says, is to form an armed militia in
the hills around Marfa. The thing to do is to attack government
installations—tax men and the like—until the governor resigns and
Texas secedes from the country.

It occurs to me, they're threatening people like my brother.

As the man speaks, he gestures stiffly, waving a sweat-darkened
straw cowboy hat.

Defiant. Hate-filled. I recognize these men. Men without
friends.

I get up to order another lemonade, but the waitress has van-
ished into a back room somewhere. I wait by the kitchen door, tap-
ping the bottom of my glass on the glass jukebox top. Jerry Jeff,
Waylon, Willie—and two surprising selections, "Satisfaction" and
"Eleanor Rigby." I pull some change from my pocket, punch up the
Beatles. The men turn to me.

Rock music. Poetry. Hair touching the tops of my ears. *Definitely* not a citizen of the Republic of Texas.

I take deliberate, slow strides past their table. "Where you from?" says one of the men. He touches my sleeve.

"Don't," I say.

"What's that?" he says.

"Don't fucking touch me."

He plucks a toothpick from his mouth.

"Your man McVeigh," I say. Wrong step? Falling, falling; air beneath my feet? Well, but I've been waiting for this moment, haven't I? "He was a pussy."

Okay, I think: it ain't Dante, but it's eloquent enough to get a rise from these old loons. "What the fuck?" says the guy who'd touched my shirt. The Beatles sigh for all the lonely people.

I wait but the fellows don't stir. They won't do it, won't make a move for me. I drop some money on my table and stroll outside. This is how I waste my days, how I waste and waste my days.

I've left my sister-in-law's book inside the café, in tatters on a wet placemat. Maybe if I lose her poet, *she'll* kick my ass when she gets back, full of the wisdom of the Old World. Make me pay. Pull the books from her shelves and bloody my face with words.

I laugh. I walk down the street laughing, unable to stop. A young mother hurries her child past me and into the safety of a dime store. That's right, ma'am. Who *knows* who I am? Just another stranger in town.

"But what's he *laughing* at?" I hear the child plead, just inside the store.

I slip into an alley and slump against a Dumpster until I recover my senses. The sun hammers my face.

What just happened? I think.

Why am I here? Why am I still here, when the tongues of others could say so much more, so much better than I ever will?

I remember laughing with my brother when he first moved to Marfa—going off the highway, out into the desert, to see the ruins of the *Giant* movie set, the old, worn bones of the house where Liz and Rock Hudson played at bigger-than-life happiness. Broken windows. Steps leading nowhere. "*Giant* country will be a new start for Jenny and me," Bo said. "A rescue." And it was. The boy never gave up, chasing joy. I don't know how he does it. "The bad old times—Dad, the miscarriage, the jobs, losing Mom—well," he said. "Hundreds of years ago. Long forgotten. We've been punished enough, little brother. And for what? For Christ's sake, what mistakes did we make?" We talked about car rides. Ice chips. We laughed like we laughed as kids, like we hadn't laughed since. I almost believed him when he talked about the future. Wind blew through the empty old house.

Now I wipe dusty tears from my face, brush the dirt from my pants. I feel my two good legs, the strength of my arms. The Border Patrol truck chugs past, kicking up more dust. The driver still wears his steel helmet. Through small glass panes in the truck's rear door I glimpse two frightened faces, boys ten or eleven years old.

A low growl. Faraway thunder. It won't amount to anything. Like yesterday, the day before, and the day before that. Tomorrow, the sun will do what it always does. In town, the buildings will stand firm against the wind, and it'll be easy to find some shade.

The Inhalatorium

Robert's father, a geologist, told him that West Texas was once underwater. A vast ocean resided here, he said. It receded over centuries, leaving behind the nutrients that feed the varieties of plant life we find today in the desert, and accounting for the flatness of the land.

"Maybe you're part fish," Robert's father kidded him whenever Robert fell prey to an asthma attack, usually in the middle of the night, waking from sleep. "Maybe that explains your breathing trouble."

Robert's mother, a heavy smoker who'd developed her nicotine habit early, had died of emphysema when he was a baby. On nights when he couldn't breathe, there was only his father to sit with him, rub his back, and hum a song until he fell asleep again.

"Sometimes," his father would say, kneeling beside Robert's bed, "the world is less than splendid. But don't give up on it, okay?"

"Okay," Robert answered. He wasn't sure what "splendid" meant, but the implication was that Robert's mother was one of the weak ones who had given up on life. All that was left of her was the chandelier she had bought for the dining room before he was born, its sharp glass diamonds yellowed from years of cigarette and candle smoke rising from the table.

Robert was twenty-two, and twelve credits shy of a bachelor's degree in American history, when his father passed away of congestive heart failure, a condition that caused excess fluid in the lungs. Saddened and distracted, Robert took a year off from college to travel in the desert, in memory of his father and his work. He'd familiarize himself with the region's contours and surprises: a way of keeping the old man's spirit with him a little longer. He washed and waxed his father's silver Pontiac, and tuned it up for the rigors of the trip.

He put the family house on the market, and left the details of the sale to a real estate agent. On his last day in town, Robert stood in the dining room with the woman, taking stock, making sure he'd packed everything he wanted. "That's a beautiful old chandelier," said the agent, nodding at the ceiling. She was pretty and thin, like Robert's mother in scrapbook photographs.

"Yes," Robert said. Here, as a child, on the dining room floor night after night, he'd sat looking up at his father as his father served supper, usually steak and sweet potatoes. Robert stared out the window, at a perfectly oval beehive just beneath the eave of the house (it hung there like a brittle chandelier). He'd played with his black and white Manx. Katia had never learned to retract her claws when she sparred with him. Robert still had cat-scars, whitened now, and hard, on his arms.

"It'll be here long after we're gone," the agent said, admiring the cut glass.

"Yes," Robert said. He turned to shake her hand.

"Nothing to worry about," she told him.

"Yes," he said again, taking one last look around, one last full breath in the house.

On his first day out, in a men's room in a roadside rest area just north of the Texas-Mexico border, Robert read a faded lyric on the wall:

> *Clickety clack, clickety clack.*
> *Where you going, where you been?*
> *Clickety clack, clickety clack.*
> *Don't come back, don't come back.*

Later that afternoon, tracing a route laid out on a tourist map, he saw the remnants of an outpost where Robert E. Lee had once trained to be an army general. He saw a glass and metal structure built in the late nineteenth century by a man named Will Pruett, whose goal, said the free informational literature, was to "aid sick humanity." The structure, an "Inhalatorium," had been designed for consumptives. They would stand inside it and breathe medicinal vapors. The Inhalatorium was an economic failure, said the brochures, and closed before its effectiveness as a health treatment could be determined.

As he studied the contraption—a tall glass tube in the middle of an old ravine—Robert fell into conversation with a fellow tourist who, it turned out, had suffered from asthma all his life. He laughed when Robert told him his father's old joke. "Well, maybe there's some truth to that fish business," said the man.

Together, they marveled at the fact that a whole generation had vanished from the planet, wars had been won and lost, since Will Pruett had fashioned the Inhalatorium, yet here it stood. A fragile glass booth. "Like an empty aquarium," the man remarked.

Robert was really interested in the desert's history, he said, he should read a book titled *Commerce of the Prairies*. It had been published in 1844 by a consumptive named Josiah Gregg. "It's the most eye-opening account of this region I've ever found," the man explained. "Gregg came to Texas because he thought the desert air would be good for his lungs. His book convinced hundreds of asthmatics, and people suffering from pleurisy and the like, to migrate here. Naturally, none of them ever got well." The fellow laughed again. "So. It seems a flock of invalids shaped Texas's destiny as much as the battle of the Alamo."

A few days later, Robert discovered a reprint of Josiah Gregg's book in a used bookstore and read it as he continued his travels through craggy moraines and dry fossil beds. In the West, it is "most usual to sleep out in the open air," Gregg wrote, "for the serene sky affords the most agreeable and wholesome canopy" and "seems to affect the health rather favorably."

In one of the textbooks Robert had tossed into the trunk of the car (next to his father's maps, which he no longer had the heart to look at), he read that Stephen F. Austin, one of Texas's early political leaders, had once proclaimed the "climate of Texas . . . to be decidedly superior in point of health and salubrity to any portion of North America in the same parallel."

Like Austin and Gregg, Robert's father had been an enthusiast for the region. He had always encouraged Robert to look carefully and appreciate what he saw, so he'd know the character of the place that had shaped him. No doubt Robert's passion for history had sprung from his father's excitement.

Utopians, men like this. But paradise is not a fertile, forested place, Robert thought. Fertility breeds fevers and disease. Instead, perfection is a desiccated emptiness.

This notion troubled Robert's sleep, especially when his daily drive left him far from towns, and he was forced to bed down in the car or on the ground. When he did sleep he dreamed of dark and empty distances. No movement, sound, or air.

The world was perfect. It was paradise. We decided to change it.
These words swam through Robert's mind just before sleep one night, after he had spent nearly an hour reading Josiah Gregg's book. Robert was staying in the Cactus Glory Motel, just off the Alpine highway. Tires hissed on the road outside his window. Coyotes called in the cooling night air.

After several minutes he drifted. The book fell to the floor. He startled awake, chasing his breath, which floated just out of reach. He coughed, choked, stumbled to the window and opened its latch. A mild wind flowed into the room. It filled Robert's lungs like water pouring into two tall jars. *Will this sustain me*, he thought, *or is this my last taste of the world?* He leaned as far as he could into the night.

The following morning, a warm wind blew in from Mexico, stirring dust devils in the road, coloring the air a thick, chalky brown. Radio weathermen predicted a rough week ahead. The scars on Robert's arms—Katia's old love-marks—itched as he drove (windows up or down, it didn't matter) through the hard and grainy heat.

Because of his weak lungs, Robert had always expected to die young. And yet, whenever breath left him, he was shocked. "Trauma," a doctor said to him once. "The loss of a loved one. Disappointments. They seem to trigger asthma. We're not sure why."

Well, Robert thought. When the world reveals itself as less than splendid, why keep taking it in?

"Often, people don't realize how serious asthma can be," the doctor went on.

But don't give up, right?

He stood before a prickly pear cactus next to the highway. At its base, pink and blue flowers.

Robert was waiting for his car, which had overheated on the road, to stop steaming. He would have to find some water.

Meanwhile, he studied the cactus and the flowers: had they evolved from ocean plants? This was not the landscape people envisioned when they thought of the Garden of Eden. But isn't it true, he asked himself, that most of us picture a garden when we think of paradise?

In the last few days, he had been stopping at small-town libraries and reading old newspapers in the archives, continuing the story where Josiah Gregg left off: articles about hackers and coughers on a limping pilgrimage to the West. Over the decades, they had been accompanied by treasure hunters, railroad magnates, entrepreneurs, electricians, and oil workers. In 1999, the *Los Angeles Times* reported that Phoenix, Arizona, had become so swollen with people, doctors had coined a new term, "Valley Fever," for illnesses caused by pathogens in the dirt stirred up by continuous human activity. Fatigue. Fungus in the bones and brain.

"Everybody who lives here has a health problem," said one Phoenix resident.

Apparently, the snake had followed each fresh young Adam and Eve to every new garden. Paradise, no longer seductive . . .

The Pontiac sputtered and let out a sigh, the kind of rattle his father had made in the hospital in the last stages of his illness. Robert turned and looked at the car. Sweat stung the scars on his arms. He went for a jug of water.

The winds grew stronger. One afternoon, in a town called Salton, Robert stopped at a pharmacy. He had been wheezing so badly he couldn't hear the car radio. He had caught only parts of a newscast that said the dust in the air was thickened by smoke from a forest fire north of Oaxaca.

"Don't sound so good," said the pharmacist, a bald man with wire-rimmed glasses pressed tightly to his face.

Fluids moved through Robert's chest. He scanned the shelves for inhalers.

"Strongest medicine's on the top shelf. Albuterol. Green box," the man said.

Robert brought it to the counter, along with a bag of pretzels and a canned Coke.

"No sir, don't sound good at all," the man said.

Just a taste of what's ahead, Robert thought.

Above the cash register, a small glass chandelier cast weak light on the sales counter and the floor.

"Well, take care, young fellow. Awful nasty out there, with the wind and all."

"I'm good," Robert said. "Thanks."

The light fixture sang three high notes as he opened the door and a breeze caught the swaying glass pendants.

• • • •

That night, Robert unrolled his sleeping bag on a dirt patch several miles off the road. As the night darkened, the Milky Way spread like powdered glass above the land.

He remembered a camping trip he had taken with his father. He must have been six, maybe seven: one of his earliest rides into the desert with his dad. They had pitched their bedrolls at the bottom of a warm canyon. The air was still. Later that night, Robert shot to his feet, gasping. His father lifted him, pounding his back, toward anything he could suck for strength.

Afterward, his father had sat and showed him maps, to humor him and keep him calm. "Never give up," his father said. "No matter what. There's always a road out, you understand?"

Smiling at the memory, Robert crossed his arms behind his head. He stared at the stars. A silver satellite drifted across the Big Dipper's bowl. Another movement: a bit of space junk, a second satellite, a silent jet?

No. The object, a single mass made of many parts, dropped several feet and danced above the ground. The hair stood stiff on Robert's arms. He swore it was . . . it seemed to be . . .

The image broke apart. Flashing slivers wriggled in the air, illuminated by a cheddar-yellow moon.

Robert sat up. "All right," he said aloud. "I'm dreaming. This is a dream and I know it's a dream. I'm going to lie down and dream of something else. My father and me on the lawn, running, playing catch. Katia leaping behind us. Mother watching from the kitchen."

He lay back and closed his eyes. "Dream," he whispered. What he thought he had seen was a school of blue and yellow fish, darting out at him from the constellation Lyra.

• • • •

He had lost track of the days of the week. He only understood it was Sunday when he heard hymns from a church down the road as he stood filling his tank with gas. After he paid the service station attendant, a high school kid wearing a "Ski El Paso" T-shirt, Robert drove half a block and parked the car in a small dirt lot.

He walked to the church and stood on the concrete porch, peering into the open doorway. In a cool, shaded vestibule, a middle-aged woman slouched against a wall, smoking. In her left hand, she held a gold aluminum ashtray, stuffed with butts. The woman nodded at Robert and went on puffing. It was hard for him not to stare at the ashtray, at the smeared lipstick on the tips of the crushed cigarettes. He turned his head to see inside the chapel, but it was dark, with just a few candles, and so long as he stood in the sunlight his eyes would not adjust to the shade.

"We will come to understanding by and by," someone said—presumably the preacher. Robert remembered hearing the phrase years ago. His father had not been a churchgoer—"Too much the scientist," he'd say whenever Robert asked him why he never talked of God—but he had taken Robert to Mass a few times when Robert was little, thinking, perhaps, that in the absence of his mother the boy needed solace that a working father couldn't offer. Robert recalled sitting in the sanctuary puzzling over the phrase "by and by." Did it mean *next to, because of,* or *all in good time?*

Next to the beehive, through repeated, stinging pain, I learned of loss, Robert thought.

Because of my parents' illnesses, I learned of loss.

All in good time, from traveling and leaving things behind, I've learned about loss.

The smoking woman smiled at him again. He had been staring at her without realizing it. He glanced at his hands, at the lines in his palms. What are you hoping to find? he thought. He rubbed his hands as if to smooth a map.

The flare of a match. A sulfurous smell. The woman kissed another cigarette.

The dreams came almost every night now. Gills, whirring blue fins, yellow tails, inches from the ground.

Robert told himself to wake up. None of this was real. He sat stiffly in his sleeping bag, wheezing, hugging his backpack to his chest. He rubbed his eyes and shined his flashlight into the dust until the last of the fish disappeared.

"So far, three couples have looked at the house," the real estate agent told him on the phone. "I think one of them may make an offer." Her voice rang high, like a child's, but he remembered how much she looked like his mother. As he slouched in the phone booth, watching teenagers in muddy cars circle a burger joint across the highway, he imagined holding a conversation he never could have had. In his mind, his mother sat in the dining room, beneath the chandelier, wearing a light cotton dress.

"So the house is good?" he said.

"Terrific," said his mother. Confident. Healthy.

"And the lawn?"

"Glorious. I'll be sure to water it again this evening."

"I'm glad."

"Nothing to worry about. Nothing at all."

None of this is real.

"I'll let you know if an offer comes through, okay?"

"Okay," Robert said.

Across the road, cars went round and round.

As days passed, he feared his mother's spirit had taken possession of the Pontiac, and of him, blowing him aimlessly down paths narrow and obscure. You'll never return, he thought. What's left for you to reclaim?

Abandoned studies of the past.

A house no longer yours.

He hacked. Wheezed. A splendid surrender.

While searching for a place to sit and eat a sandwich, Robert came upon the bones of a bird, tiny as grass clippings, tangled in thorny brush. The bones reminded him of a discovery he had made when he was twelve, out looking for his cat. Katia had been missing for hours, and Robert's father feared an owl might have snatched her. Lately, some of the neighbors had spotted a Great Horned— "unusual but not entirely rare in this part of the world," Robert's father had said.

Sure enough, in the alley behind the house, Robert found bone and hair in a ball: an owl's regurgitations. Robert placed the remains in a pickle jar, like the one in which his father kept his "rainy day" coins. He carried the jar to his room. His father had returned to his office after dinner, to work with his maps. Robert set the jar on a windowsill and crouched before it as the moon rose. Yellow light trailed across the contours of the glass, across the hardened ball: his ex-cat. Robert stared, as if this moment, this image, might reveal to him life's liquid motion, the changes, the futures embodied in us all—futures we never saw unless we paused and really looked.

Now, he gazed at the bird's remains. Maybe Katia and this poor flying creature were lucky to leave the world before their bodies betrayed them.

His chest ached. Years ago, a doctor had told him he was using only 10 percent of his lung capacity. "I have half a mind to hospitalize you," the doctor had said.

Robert felt now as he had felt back then, and he knew he'd become dependent on the inhaler. Its effectiveness was eroding. Perhaps he should buy a new one, or maybe even see a doctor in the next town.

On the outskirts of Marfa, Robert sat at a red light. Up and down the street, air-conditioners clattered in windows, allowing people to live in this place where otherwise they would perish.

> *Clickety clack, clickety clack.*
> *Don't come back, don't come back.*

He saw a sign for an allergy and asthma specialist. The office was closed. He would return in the morning. The inhaler did nothing for him now. Too much dust. Too much smoke and wind.

He passed a small crowd off the road. They had gathered to see the Marfa Lights, erratic and mysterious flashes in the sky. In a brochure he'd read that the lights had become a tourist draw: some folks believed they were evidence of alien spacecraft; others called them spirits of the dead. Sober-minded observers insisted they were car lights reflected by dust-grains, or traces of glowing swamp gas.

Robert kept going. He turned onto a deserted farm road. Finally, he stopped and spread his sleeping bag in an open field surrounded by mesquite. His wheezing silenced the crickets. He pulled his flashlight and *Commerce of the Prairies* out of his backpack. He tried to read, but the words floated off the page. All right. He was exhausted. Dizzy from lack of oxygen. Nothing to worry about. Nothing at all. He'd go to the specialist in the morning.

He dozed, and woke to find his flashlight losing juice. He shook it. Inside, the batteries rattled like fingernails tapping a pane of glass.

He slept again and dreamed of the fish.

When he woke, he was encased inside the Inhalatorium.

Water filled the desert.

"This is ridiculous. I'm dreaming," he said aloud. His voice echoed in the jar. He said no more, for fear of burning up oxygen.

Tap. Tap tap. He turned to see his mother swaying in the water in a splendid green dress. Young and strong. Behind her, a glass chandelier rose in midair, as majestic as a jellyfish. He kissed his mother's fingers through the glass. Katia bobbed past, trailed by exotic plankton. Then Robert's father tumbled into view, weightless and thin. He waved something—a map: the word "Paradise" stamped across its top.

Robert mouthed the words, "I did it." He meant to say, *I've done as you said, Father. I saw where I came from.* His father tried to straighten the map. The night's currents slowed his hands but he wouldn't give up. Watching him, Robert understood, with a swell of excitement and fear, where he'd been headed all along. *Ocean and desert. Sea and sky.* Soon, he was going to run out of air.

Observations of Bumblebee Activity during the Solar Eclipse, June 30, 1954

being a rough and unexpurgated draft of my report to the Academy, containing a note of explanation to you . . . don't worry, Hans, I'll edit before submitting.—A. L.

Our goal was to see if bumblebees seek blossoms in unexpected darkness. The observations took place at the Biological Station near Bergen (sixty degrees north, five degrees east), well within the path of the total eclipse. The observers were Hans Lyme (Observer A) from the University of Bergen, and me, Amy Locke (Observer B), a postdoctoral student from Santa Fe, New Mexico, in the southwestern United States.

From early morning the day was gray and dull, and severely restricted insect activity. Afterward, I realized that the conditions, with nearly constant temperature and humidity, leaving light intensity as the only variable of consequence, formed a favorable outdoor laboratory—more so than if the sky had been clear.

Rubus idaeus L was the plant identified for inspection. Two areas of wild-growing bushes, still in fairly good bloom, were selected (after much back-and-forth between Observers A and B about the optimal atmosphere for gathering data and for pursuing amorous prankishness, Observer A being notoriously distracted in the field). Eventually, sites were chosen from the point of view of best bumblebee activity; five meters apart, the bushes were situated on a rather steep hillock, exposed to the south and a steady southerly wind.

The observers synchronized their watches (this took longer than expected, as, during the process, Observer A became increasingly enamored of Observer B's left wrist). Observations were made by turning our heads right to left, counting every *Bombus* in range (Observer B ignoring the frequent—and hilariously charming—"Yoo-hoos" rising from Observer A's reedy perch). Temperature and humidity were measured by means of a Lambrecht's psychrometer Number 740. Light intensity was measured by means of a sixtomat from the top of a hill (altitude approximately twenty meters). According to Observer A, elevated heart rate caused by glimpses, through the bushes, of Observer B's exposed and milky ankles, was beyond calculation.

All pertinent findings may be regarded as accurate enough for the purposes of this report.

Though bumblebee activity was minimal all day, it declined as the eclipse progressed, and individual bees—apart from one specimen in Observer B's immediate vicinity—had disappeared by totality. The remaining specimen was heard for another minute but of course could not be seen owing to darkness.

(. . . and then you were upon me, stinging my mouth with kisses, my thighs bared to the brisk southerly winds.

Hans, forgive me for not responding, but with the sudden

death of my brother last month [though it had been apparent for some time that he had fallen from the nest, away from his healthy fellows], and the rakish reputation preceding you, I had decided, just that morning, to forgo my studies and my professional ambitions, and return to my home desert. The gloom I felt in the field that day surpassed the shade all around us. In the desert, little grows so nothing is hidden. It can be strangely refreshing. Mentally clarifying. A phenomenon worthy of research.)

Shortly after totality, the temperature declined. This drop may be explained by increasing wind, followed by a series of light afternoon showers. There is reason to believe that neither the slight variation of the humidity nor the very short periods of drizzle had an influence on bumblebee activity.

It ought to be mentioned that under normal conditions bee behavior in this climate is usually constant throughout the day.

The only remaining problem left for this discussion (besides the eternal puzzles of disease and life cut short, of inappropriate laughter and love budding at the least likely moments) is the fact that, while a few bees continued to work the blossoms in the darkness, nearly nine minutes elapsed before the full contingent returned to the field following the eclipse. This confirms previous sightings indicating that bees need a certain level of illumination before starting their dances. Temperature is usually believed to be the limiting factor that delays fieldwork in the morning in spite of sufficient light intensity. Our eclipse observations—made while the temperature was nearly constant—suggest that other factors may be at work.

(A kiss on my naked back between the shoulder blades, to ease the pain of a sudden bite; my tears, which I could not explain to you at the time. So many factors beyond the fine calibrations of our instruments.)

The wind speed rose immediately after the total eclipse, but only to a rate that normally has no influence on group behavior. Naturally, deteriorating conditions make more challenging any attempt, on our part, to understand individuals.

Concluding remarks:

1. If we presume that the total eclipse made the bees return to their nests, the time that passed before they retook the field may be explained as the normal time needed before starting another trip. (A cone of shadow spreading before me: endless trips to silent, empty rooms.)

2. The specimen who remained in the field may be presumed to be naturally wan (like flatland dust, like my little brother in the months before he slipped away); it cannot be proved that the eclipse had any effect on him whatsoever. Before the eclipse, certain sluggish individuals were observed hugging the bushes. The "specimen" bee may have been one of these. (Though his bite certainly had vigor! Your surprising kiss, so delicate and caring. Listlessness seems to be *my* new permanent state, Hans. Torpor: the desert temperament. Forgive me. Along with grief, it is something I must try to overcome. I hope you can excuse my abrupt good-bye, and prosper in your studies with liveliness, humor, and relish.)

3. There is no reason to discuss these problems any further. Apidologists have long been aware of the behaviors of *Bombus pratorum* described herein, but as far as I know

have never been given such convincing proof of them. I am pleased to have made some small contribution to the field before leaving it for good, in stricken self-exile—how *does* one survive the darkness?—and for further information I refer my fellow sufferers (scratch that—fellow *students*) to the accompanying diagrams.

Bern

E very evening at 5:30, Bern walked from the storefront office of
the small architectural firm he worked for on West Eighth Street
to Glasco's, a bar one block north of the Cedar Tavern on University
Place. There he had a sandwich and a beer. After dining alone in the
melancholy comfort of noisy anonymity, he strolled along West
Eleventh in the direction of the river, taking in the mild midwinter
night. The steel gratings in the walls of the old brownstones emitted
blasts of hot air smelling oddly of hair oil. Through the street-level
basement windows of the First Presbyterian Church (sooty Gothic
Revival), he glimpsed women sweating over an industrial stove.

A few paces later, Bern prickled at the bland modern facade facing the street where anarchists blew up their 1840s-era townhouse
in the 1970s. These days, the front window of the first floor showcased a teddy bear dressed in a yellow slicker, holding a black
umbrella—the occupant's wink (Bern assumed) to the
Weathermen, the group that had built the bomb.

A young man marched past Bern, hoisting a boy onto his
shoulders. "Mommy's *stressed*," the man warned the boy. Mommy
was nowhere in sight.

The sidewalk, a mix of new and old concrete squares, displayed slopes and dips. In the bare little garden of PS 41, a black and broken umbrella lay on the ground. A bearded man in a heavy coat and a Mets cap climbed over a rail fence onto the school property, gripping a plastic trash bag, and began searching for scraps among the garden's twigs.

Usually, Bern stopped at the end of the block to contemplate the Wall of Hope and Remembrance on the south side of St. Vincent's Hospital. Hundreds of notes and photos commemorated people never found after the attack on the World Trade Center. On the sidewalk, someone had left a child's light blue sweater and a pair of baby shoes. Pigeons cooed in the building's concrete eaves.

Bern was startled to find the brick wall blank, emptied of its elegiac icons. A siren shrieked. An ambulance pulled up to the curb. From its rear, two paramedics unloaded a man on a stretcher.

Still dazed by the hard, cold wall, Bern turned from the hospital's emergency entrance. Across the street, in the front window of a shop called Fantasy World, faceless mannequins lounged, wearing sheer pink lingerie. Down the block, wind ruffled the red canvas awning of the Village Vanguard. Bern shuffled up the street to the White Horse, where he stopped for another beer.

At a table next to him, two women were in conversation:

"How's her father?"

"*Which* father?"

"I know, I know . . ."

Someone had left part of the *Times*, wet and rumpled, on a chair. Distractedly, Bern raced through the paper. Why did the hospital's cleared wall disturb him? He had not known anyone who died in the attack. From the beginning, he had resisted the media call to public mourning and the government's shameless fear-mongering.

Here, now, was a headline declaring that Governor Spitzer had signed off on the Freedom Tower. A mistake, Bern thought. Who would occupy the thing? It was terribly designed.

He finished his beer and paid. His agitation—over what?—was too great for sleep, so he walked some more, retracing his steps. He ducked into the Strand.

"Was Ishmael the whale," he heard someone say, "or the guy that tried to kill the whale, or—?"

On the table of New York titles, Bern found a reprint of E. B. White's *Here Is New York*, a volume he had loved twenty years ago as a fresh arrival on the island, straight out of college, though even then the book had had a musty air about it. White's New York was that of the Beaux Arts urban canyons of the 1920s and 1930s, full of brick buildings with cozy window ledges and niches that sheltered restless doves: a city long vanished. Since 9/11, White's book was spoiled for Bern because its prophetic conclusion—"A single flight of planes no bigger than a wedge of geese can quickly end this island fantasy"—had been quoted so often in the press and in the blogosphere.

On the shelves Bern found a pristine paperback entitled *A Hut of One's Own* by a woman named Ann Cline. On impulse he decided to buy it. He liked the cover illustration: a black-and-white photo of a simple square table, a kerosene lantern, a pitcher and a pan, all in a small wooden room. Like most old-school (i.e., middle-aged) architects he knew, Bern was fond of huts—of the *idea* of the hut.

He hiked to Seventh and caught the subway, then darted over to West Twenty-third Street. His apartment was on the fourth floor of a building with wide glass doors, next to a new thrift shop called McGee's, whose sign was painted to appear beat-up, old, and faded.

In the lobby of his building, a worn blue carpet that had once been plush—ten, fifteen years ago—kinked like popcorn beneath his shoes as he moved toward the elevator. A dull, gassy odor filled the lobby, rising from the sofa squeezed against the far wall between two potted ficus plants with cobwebs stretched among their leaves. The smell came from old leather that had been too much in contact with soiled clothing over the years—the sweaty dresses and slightly damp bottoms of long-forgotten visitors to the building.

A hand-drawn map of Paterson, New Jersey, now mostly faded, was framed on the wall above the sofa, next to a chipped mirror whose smoky, yellowed glass flattered even a weary Bern after a trying day. Its smudged spots smoothed the lines under his eyes and seemed to straighten his mildly crooked nose. On the sofa slept Mrs. Mehl, about whom Bern knew little. Widow. Third floor. Light snorer, often asleep here in the evening. Tonight there were two bags of groceries—cat food and chocolate cookies sticking out—on the floor at her feet, as if she had made it just this far, surviving the bustle on the streets, and could walk no more.

Gently, Bern nudged her shoulder, nearly lost in the padding of a purple coat. "Mrs. Mehl. Dear," he said. "You'll want to go up now. It's getting late."

"Oh yes, yes. Certainly," she said, primping her sparse white hair as if she hadn't been napping but was prepping backstage, somewhere, for her moment in the klieg lights.

"Can I help you with your bags?"

"No, no. Well, just the one, perhaps. Thank you," said Mrs. Mehl, and they rode the lift together in mute dignity. When the doors, heavy wood with copper trim, sighed apart, Mrs. Mehl wrestled the bag from Bern's arms, thanked him again, and swiftly turned the corner in the dim, greenly lighted hallway. Bern smelled leaden fried foods—perhaps pork chops and onions? And he also detected some rare Asian leaf. Was it Kaffir lime?

In his apartment, he added water to a blue vase on his kitchen counter that held a single moss rose—a reminder of his East Texas childhood, just outside of Houston, where moss roses grew in abundance. He switched on his bedside radio. Another car bomb in Baghdad. Another condemnation by the vice president of war critics, whom he implied were traitors to our brave and steadfast republic.

Before turning off his light, Bern flipped through Ann Cline. "St. Anthony in a hut, immobile in the face of worldly temptations," he read. The hut was the "tap-root of inhabiting."

Bern closed the book and lay in the humid dark. Cline's remarks reminded him of Carlo Lodoli, an eighteenth-century Venetian architect he had learned about in grad school. Apparently, Lodoli had much to say about wood, stone, and bone, and their uses in construction. Bern remembered that, in addition to promoting radical building designs, Lodoli was suspected by the Inquisitors of the Republic of spreading seditious ideas. Upon his death, officials confiscated his papers, including his architectural jottings, and locked them away under a leaky roof in the Piombi, where they rotted. Only through the subsequent, and much embellished, writings of his students, Algarotti and Memmo, did Lodoli's thoughts survive, as rumor, hint, and innuendo.

Back in school, Bern had deduced that the master's teachings, if they could ever properly be known, argued that the point of architecture was to understand the nature of the materials it employed. Perhaps this is what disturbed me earlier, Bern thought now. Isn't the aim of all human activity—violence, remembrance—to plumb human activity? Tap roots. First principles. So damnably hard to trace.

● ● ● ●

He had not visited the WTC site in five years. Early this morning,
before heading to work, he felt a desire to see the area again. On the
subway he stared at the cover of the Ann Cline book. The table, the
pitcher, the pan.

Of course, there was not much to see at the site. A vast construction zone, with little construction in progress. Pataki's Pit,
everyone called it, deriding the former governor's politics, which
had kept the hole a hole longer than it needed to be.

Bern was not as pleased as he thought he would be by the new
structure—knife-edged and opaque—on the pit's north lip: 7
World Trade Center, the newspaper reviews of which had been
mostly positive. To Bern, the building's blocky base screamed *fear*.
The first ten floors housed an electrical substation that powered
most of Lower Manhattan. But did it have to *look* like an electrical
substation? Bern mused. The Jenny Holzer installation—a series of
ghostly words marching across the front glass wall, including lines
from *Here Is New York* and celebrations of the city from the poems
of Walt Whitman—charmed him but left him feeling irritated that
he couldn't stay all morning to read it.

Bern made his way past Vietnamese street vendors hawking
New York sweatshirts and woolen caps, as well as pamphlets with
TRAGEDY printed in red across the top.

Bern's office on West Eighth was small and drab, outfitted only
with a desk, a rarely used computer, a few chairs, and a smattering
of file cabinets overflowing with paperwork. The dirty windows
overlooked a secondhand clothing store. Usually at lunch, Bern left
the building, passed through the dreary lobby—almost always
empty—caught a subway, and strolled up to Madison Square Park.

There, under the pleasant shadows of curling oak trees, he'd eat a sandwich he'd packed at home.

Today, he worked into the early afternoon on a project for a small foundation whose office space on West Broadway lacked sufficient light in the interior, despite floor-to-ceiling windows facing the street. Where Bern would normally place tubing for a light scoop, an old fire escape interfered—a pretty little problem that kept him from fully realizing his hunger until well past midday. When he *did* knock off for a while, he walked and stretched, ending up at a nice little Italian place on West Eleventh called Gene's. While he waited for his salad, he sketched hut designs on his napkin: flat-roofed, pyramid-shaped, open to the air.

He took a meandering path back to work. Children's drawings of the neighborhood filled the front window of Ray's Pizza: happy families clustered beneath the Jefferson Market Library clock or around the flower garden where the women's prison used to stand (long before the children could have known about it).

For three more hours he worked on the foundation design. At 5:30 he wandered over to Glasco's, to find it locked and dark. A handwritten sign taped to the front window cited plumbing problems and apologized for the inconvenience. A tall young woman in jeans and a green wool sweater stepped up beside him, squinted to read the sign, stepped back, and gripped the straps of her tan leather purse tightly against her body. Bern recollected having seen her in Glasco's now and then.

"Well," she said. "I guess it's the Cedar tonight." She set off down the street, her auburn hair bouncing on her shoulders. After a moment's delay, Bern followed her.

The only seats inside the tavern were jammed into a corner. Bern squeezed next to the woman in green. "May I?" he asked. She answered, "Sure." Separately, they ordered drinks and food. The place was too bright. Acoustically bad.

Bern scribbled on his napkin.

After a few sips of her beer—Guinness, Bern noted; this woman was serious about her beer—she said to Bern, "Nice," and indicated the napkin with a lift of her chin. "Are you an artist?"

"No."

"Make houses?"

"I'm an architect, yes."

"Cool," she said. She drank some more. "Say something . . . I don't know . . . architecturally *cool*."

Bern laughed. She had a way of speaking loudly, over the crowd, which sounded soft: the low timbre of her voice, perhaps. "Well, I'm not sure I . . ."

"Come on. Amuse me. It's been a long day."

"Okay. Let's see. The seventeenth-century Jesuit, Athanasius Kircher, attributed to demons all of Roman architecture, because of the nudity in its statuary," Bern said.

"No kidding?"

"The philosopher Vico believed that the bastard children of Noah's sons became giants by feeding on the nitrates in their own feces, which they rolled around in—primitives that they were—and that their large stature and fat fingers led to crude and awkward building practices."

"You're something else," the woman said. "I'm Kate."

"Wally. Wally Bern."

"So, Wally, what are these little houses all about?" She tapped the napkin, leaving two or three wet spots on it. "Is this how architects doodle?"

Their sandwiches arrived and Bern swept the napkin into his

lap. "I suppose, periodically, most professionals seek a renewal," he said, aware of his shyness, his formal speech. "A return to first principles, right? When the business starts to feel stale or the ideas dry up. We try to remember what drew us to our work in the first place—that initial euphoria, the falling-in-love—and we reach back to basics."

"Sure," Kate said. "When you get in a rut."

"Yes. Well, in my profession, the hut is often seen as the most basic building design. The source: column and roof. The idea that it must have been raining the day Adam and Eve left paradise. They had a sudden need for shelter, you see, so they grabbed the first things they could find. Tree limbs for structural support, leaves and grasses for their ceiling."

"Cool," Kate said.

"There's something very appealing, very elegant, about the *spare.*"

"So." She brushed foam from her lips. "Your ideas are stale, huh?"

"Excuse me?"

"These doodles. Back to basics. You're feeling a need for renewal?"

Bern wiped his mouth with the napkin. Kissing the hut, he thought. Falling in love once more. "I'm not sure. The truth is . . ." Did he really want to explain? To someone just killing time after work? "I've been thinking, in the last day or so, about the wrangling over the World Trade Center site—the rebuilding process, you know, the *meaning* of it—how we've lost sight of the basic needs for that area, our community values."

"Like?"

He didn't know *what* he wanted to say. Why had he babbled on so? "We have a fundamental desire to understand what happened there and why, so whatever we do with it should involve, I think, first principles."

"Wally? You want to put a *hut* at Ground Zero?"

Bern stared at her.

"Well, well. You are *crazy*, baby." She ate her sandwich.

Did he believe what he had told the woman at dinner? He hadn't said so many words—to anyone—in weeks. Nerves. The unexpected break in his evening routine. The loss of the Wall of Hope and Remembrance.

A need for renewal?

He walked and walked, all the way up to Bryant Park, past the statues of Goethe and Gertrude Stein, then back down to the Strand. The E. B. White book still sat, prominently displayed, on a table near the front entrance. Next to it, Henry James's *The American Scene*. Bern picked it up. Published in 1907. After a twenty-year sojourn in Europe, James had returned to New York to find its "Gothic" pride "caged and dishonoured" by "buildings grossly tall and grossly ugly." Some of these, Bern knew, were the Beaux Arts beauties White would find charming, but for James they were filled with too many windows, which ruined their "grace."

New York's style had changed, wholesale, at least twice—if such a thing could even be measured—since James had first observed it. Bern made his way over to Twenty-third Street, taking another circuitous route past the Flatiron Building, past Edith Wharton's birthplace—an old Anglo-Italian brownstone—and the Chelsea Hotel. At home, he tried to read himself to sleep. "Sweet, sacred, and profane"—this is the "hut dream," said Ann Cline.

In the street in front of McGee's someone yelled obscenities. "She don't *want* my skinny brown ass no more!" another man barked into a cell phone. A car horn brayed.

Bern closed his eyes and tried to picture a garden, a soothing space in which he could slumber, but various thoughts intruded: E. B. White, auburn hair, leaky roofs. Lodoli seems to have believed it was humanity's aim to perfect nature. Imperfect in itself, nature offered materials to men and women of genius who, in choosing certain substances for particular designs, improved the makeup of matter. In this way, the world strove to return to paradise.

Bern imagined moss roses, hoping to will himself into a dream. Acres and acres of orange and yellow blossoms around the family house and near his grandfather's grave, north of Houston: the small granite stone under swelling Gulf Coast clouds, the swoon-inducing sweetness of pollen, and the dense, rich loam underneath.

Glasco's remained closed the following evening. The plumbing sign had been removed. A new sign said, "Vacation. Back in Three Weeks." Bern suspected something more sinister at work. He had witnessed elsewhere the abrupt letting-down of clientele, as in the saga of the Gotham Book Mart, which had apparently been dying of high rent for two years now without admitting as much to its customers. No one knew the store was in trouble until the steel fencing came down in front of its windows, shutting out of reach the first-edition Joyces and the copies of *The Sun Also Rises* signed by Papa himself. Had Glasco's lost its liquor license? Had the building been sold?

The Cedar was even louder than last night. Bern didn't see an empty chair until one sailed across his sight-line, dragged by a booted foot. The foot—a lovely and perfectly functional ornament—belonged to Kate. "Okay, hut-man. I've been waiting for my turkey and mayo for thirty minutes now. I'm hungry and bored. Tell me something crazy," Kate said.

Bern sat beside her. "Well, then," he said. "All right. Have you heard of Carlo Lodoli? He was history's greatest architect. He was cursed with ambitious students who distorted his teachings. He felt—or we *think* he felt—that all architecture, even the 'primitive,' had value, but his apprentice Algarotti dismissed whole continents of builders."

"You don't say."

"There are peoples on the earth, Algarotti said, who, lacking materials or a 'certain kind of intelligence,' make their huts 'out of the bones and skins of quadrupeds and marine monsters.' It's clear he disapproves."

Kate cased the busy room. "I'm *thirsty* too," she said. "Tell me more."

"Trouble arises naturally. Pleasure has to be planned for."

With cool gray eyes Kate appraised him. "How did you spend your day, Wally?"

"Sketching, on paper—"

"Not a computer guy?"

"Not a computer guy. Sketching, on paper, methods of squeezing a light scoop past a fire escape."

"How old are you?" Kate asked. "What's the matter with computers? Oh, bless you," she said to the waitress who arrived with a pint of Guinness and took Bern's order for a pilsner.

"Forty-nine. And computers—"

"No, it's okay, I get the picture. A Luddite in love with huts. I mean, you know, a little out of touch, aren't we, Grandpa?"

"What's wrong with computers is, they minimize the hand," Bern said, trying to resist Kate's humor. This girl, he feared, could make him giddy. Unseemly, at his age. *Focus.* "Building comes from nerve-endings. Fingertips. It's all about the body. But also"—as he spoke, he twisted the cardboard coaster in perfect little circles on the tabletop, and Kate watched him, amused—"with a sketch, you can't tell just by looking at it if it predates the structure, or if it's a rendering of something already there. Drawings have this magical quality, past and future all at once. They're preposterous."

"Sorry, Wally. You lost me there," said Kate.

"*Pre* and *Post*, Before and After, all in the same word. *Pre-post-erous.* The ideal architecture."

Kate laughed.

Was she put off by him? Charmed? Bern thought the latter, but he wasn't sure. She *had* asked him, the other night, to amuse her. Now, maybe she was just being polite. At least she didn't get up to leave right away.

"Forty-nine, eh? So this 'renewal' business," Kate said. "Midlife crisis? A little late in your case, maybe."

"I don't know. What *is* a midlife crisis?" Bern said. "Something dreamed up by magazine editors, I suspect."

"But you all have one, right? Sooner or later? All you guys. Wife?"

"No.

"Girlfriend? Boyfriend?"

"No."

"When was your last affair?"

"A couple of years ago," he said before he could check himself, prompted by the easy sway of their conversation. She waited for more. "I was married for two years in my late twenties. A Texas girl who hated the East and went back home. I'm okay, you know, being alone. I like solitude."

"Sex?"

His face burned. "Well, yes."

"So what do you—"

"Are you always this forward with strangers?" Bern asked.

She smiled. "You're not a stranger. Life is short, Wally."

Her sandwich appeared, and Bern ordered a garden burger. "Okay, old friend," he said. "How did you spend *your* day?"

"I'm a staff writer for a magazine called *Theatre News*."

"I'm sorry. What I said before . . . I don't really have a gripe against editors."

"It's okay." She touched his arm. "Naturally, the old hands get the plum assignments and reviews—*Vertical Hour, The Coast of Utopia*. I get the off-off-off stuff. But last week I got to meet Wallace Shawn— the lispy guy in all those Woody Allen movies? Another Wally! That was exciting. And the editors let me do a capsule review of *Translations* over at the Biltmore—the Irish play? It's the leprechaun in me."

"Hence the Guinness?"

"Cheers." She raised her glass. "My family's roots are in Ireland. As whose aren't? Anyway, we have a small but avid readership and I write small, avid articles."

"How long have you been in Manhattan?"

"Four years."

Still a tourist on the island, as was he after twenty years. "From?" he asked.

"New Orleans." Before he could speak, she added, "I haven't been back since Katrina. I'd find it too devastating. I want to remember it the way it was."

Bern mentioned the muddy bayous of his upbringing.

"Houston! So! You and me, Wally," Kate said. "Big storms in common."

"Moss roses?"

"Oh my god! You should see, in my apartment—I couldn't get over it when I saw them for sale at a street market here. In January! How do they do that?"

"Boyfriend? Girlfriend?"

"Boyfriend. Sort of. A lighting technician over at the Beckett."

"Sort of?"

"We're . . . volatile with each other, which is sometimes good, sometimes bad. You know? So we're on-again, off-again."

Bern played with the coaster. Kate watched him. "Tell me, Wally. How's your hut?"

"You laugh," he said, "and of course it's just a fantasy. But there's a certain *rightness* to the notion."

She *did* laugh at him.

"I'm serious," he said. "A return to origins. What better place for it? And it needn't be crude—the savage *box* most people picture when they hear the word 'hut.'"

"What do you mean?"

"I mean . . ." Should he? "Where *is* your apartment, Kate? Can I walk you home? I'll show you on the way."

"Wally. Are you a weirdo-psycho-creep?"

"Not weirdo-psycho."

"No rolling in feces? That sort of thing?"

"Not lately."

"Okay. Let me finish this."

Her apartment was on West Twelfth—part of an old condo, she said, that had been partitioned into hotel rooms and rental units with community baths. On the way, she mused, "I know what your trouble is, Wally. If you're thinking about Adam and Eve and *preposterous* and giants on the earth, but you're spending your days with fire escapes, well then, you're bound to feel a bit . . ."

"Displaced?"

"Yes."

"Perhaps. And the closing of Glasco's. But—"

She laughed. "You *do* like to talk, don't you? For a quiet sort."

A silent beat. Then: "Lodoli—the guy I told you about?—he liked to walk with his apprentices, looking at buildings. He saw his 'lessons' as a series of strolls and talks—*conversatio*. His favorite mode was the allegory."

"And yours?"

"The apology, I think." He stumbled over a curb. "Among Lodoli's students were young women. Unusual for that day and time."

"Is that what *I* am tonight? Your student?"

Was she flirting? Was *he*?

"Not at all. But here," Bern said. "Here we are."

They had come to the Presbyterian Church. Bern took Kate's shoulders and positioned her in front of the grand entrance. At first, she winced at his touch, but then she seemed to settle, become malleable. "All right. Imagine this building made of wood instead of stone," he said. "Slender tree trunks framing the entry, and the arch at the top formed by flexible willow limbs, curved and tied together. Can you see it?"

"Yes!" Kate said.

"Good. And the ornamentation, the busy carvings above the doorway—like foliage. In the spring, when the rooted willows sprout new life—"

"Is *that* where the design comes from? Those Gothic monsters in Europe?"

"It's a theory. So: simple wooden construction—the hut—as prototype for our greatest creations. The echo of origins. It needs to be there, like an old message in a bottle, for anything we make to have meaning."

"At Ground Zero?"

"Anywhere," Bern said. Lodoli would object. Apparently, the lost master was anything *but* a traditionalist. Still, if you love him, you must fight him, Bern thought—how else to keep the mental conversation going?

Kate nodded at Bern but looked uncertain.

"You're cold. I'll get you home," Bern said.

They strolled quietly up West Eleventh. Near Gene's, the Italian restaurant where Bern had eaten lunch the other day, they came upon a clump of small, mossy stones just off the sidewalk. "What's this?" Kate said.

Twenty or so jagged markers in the shadows, behind a tiny iron gate. "A cemetery," Bern said. "Of the old Spanish and Portuguese synagogue. Some of the city's first Jewish immigrants are buried here. In fact, this is one of the oldest graveyards in Manhattan."

"It's lovely."

"Yes, it's a favorite spot of mine. I walk by here every day."

They squinted to read the dates on the stones. 1683. 1734. 1825.

"This plot used to be much larger," Bern explained, "but city commissioners ran a road through West Eleventh and cut it in half about 1830 or so, disturbing a few unlucky souls."

He started to point out the unusual number of relief carvings on the headstones—remarkable, given the Jewish aversion to graven images. A snipped-off flower (life cut short), the Angel of

Destruction waving a flaming sword at Gotham. He stopped himself. No more Teacher for tonight, he decided. Why *did* he go on so, hiding behind his moldy old facts? To protect his thin and shabby inner life? From what? Kate seemed to enjoy him in a smirky sort of way—her Irish tolerance for blather?—but he didn't want to press his luck. He didn't flatter himself that he was sexy; on the other hand, he didn't want her to think him just another old pedant.

A green Mystic Oil truck rumbled past them. Garbage spilled from ripped bags on the corner. A rat scurried behind a low stone wall. Bern glanced down Seventh to the Vanguard. When he had first come to the city in the early 1980s, he had spent an evening in the club listening to Woody Shaw. Shaw was dead now. So was Max Gordon, the club's old owner. Ghosts of jazz. Bern remembered Shaw's drummer as ham-handed and loud.

A man in a motorized wheelchair, hunched and smoking madly, whizzed past them, nearly knocking Kate over. Bern steadied her, touching her arm. Two men in blue cotton overcoats strolled by them. "What I'm saying is, all of our daily encounters with people, even with our friends, are essentially *financial* in nature," one man said to the other.

Kate led him up West Twelfth. She pointed to a lighted window in her building. "There. Can you see?" she said. Bern followed her gesture to the fifth or sixth story: creamy yellow light through panes of rippled glass. A wrought-iron railing just inside the window frame. Wrapped around the railing, orange blossoms. "Moss roses!" he cried.

"Welcome home," Kate said. "Thank you, Wally. For the lesson, the tour."

"I'm sorry, Kate. I get carried away. Pompous."

"It was fun."

"Sleep well."

"You too. Forget about fire escapes, just for tonight. Dream of—"

Bern pecked her cheek and backed away.

A few days later, he read in the *Times* that St. Vincent's Hospital, which had "lost money for several years," planned to demolish its current building and erect a sleeker, more efficient facility across the street. The paper cited "New York's shrinking hospital industry" and said that St. Vincent's old "maze-like layout," with some rooms dating to the 1930s, had become too expensive to heat, light, and cool.

In the early afternoon, walking up Fifth to scope out a new project he had been assigned, he noticed that a shop for skin creams and facial care now occupied the high-windowed space (with old leaded frames) where Scribner's Bookstore formerly displayed its treasures. The culture had declared its priorities: vanity over history, art, and literature.

Well, Bern thought, recalling Kate's gray eyes. On one level, hard to argue.

I like solitude. Had he really told her this? However true it was, she had tapped into a deeper reality. "Rut," she said. "You get in a rut." Loneliness had become a habit with him—a common enough malady, he supposed. Especially here. Especially now.

Kate had evened his keel. Nowadays, his melancholy over the rapid changes all around him was mitigated by the pleasure she took from the regular walks they made together, from "his knowledge," she said, "of the city's many layers."

"This talk of many layers," he said uneasily one afternoon. "There are scads of books—"

She squeezed his arm. "But you're my *personal* Baedeker."

"Me?" he thought. What about Lewis Mumford? E. B. White? But he held his tongue. That day with Kate, Bern worked assiduously to stem his commentary—he faced no such problem when on his own, but now, in her presence, he became aware that his *thinking* could be antisocial—a hostile, distancing act if it wasn't parceled out.

"Like *this* neighborhood," Kate said abruptly, tugging his sleeve.

They had turned onto Greenwich Street, between Rector and Carlisle, just south of Ground Zero. The Pussycat Lounge. A peep show, a topless bar. "Your timing is uncanny," Bern told Kate. "This is actually a very interesting area."

"I knew it!"

What was he to do? It was difficult not to recede behind lectures when she prompted him like this, encouraging his natural propensity. Like dear old Lodoli, Bern considered strolling—the cold experience of *touching buildings*—a means of learning "in blood." "You really want to know?" he said.

"Absolutely."

"From, say, the 1790s to about 1820, this was the poshest real estate in Manhattan."

"Mansions?"

"Sure."

"To-die-for clubs?"

"The 'jet set' of the eighteenth century wouldn't party anywhere else. New York City got its start here at the southern tip of the island." He waved his arm. "This was the home of the mercantile elite until waterfront shipping changed the dynamic."

"Hey, Professor," a greasy-haired man with an eight ball tattooed on his chin called to Bern from a smoky doorway, "we got lap dances from ten bucks. Your lady friend's welcome too."

Kate pressed close to Bern without actually touching him. He ignored the man's black chin. "A developer wants to tear all this out now."

"Good riddance, yes?" Kate said. "Like when they cleaned up Forty-second Street."

"Except—and there's always an exception—the building that houses the Pussycat, here, is over two hundred years old, a Federal-era townhouse and, as such, rather unique and valuable. It's the old story. The developer claims to envision a better New York—wiping out blight, hmm? The Pussycat's owner claims to want to preserve the city's rich heritage. Up to a point, both men have a legitimate position. And of course, no one's listening to the ghosts of the old well-to-do, who gave the city its start and were swept away long ago."

"What kind of ice cream do you like?" Kate asked. On most afternoons, despite her apparent interest in his stories, she had about a twenty-minute limit for his oratory.

"Plain vanilla, I'm afraid."

"I could have guessed it. Let's go. I know a place just around the corner here, and it won't be crowded this time of year."

Her bounciness, a craving for distraction that came across as somewhat desperate, convinced him that his "lessons" really did delight her—"*All* Southerners are history buffs," she said. "You've read Faulkner, right?"—and this helped Bern swallow *her* first principle: "No sex between us, okay, Wally? It's not an age deal, or anything." Bern judged her to be around twenty-five—she wouldn't come right out and say. "It's just that, what with Gary"—her man "sort of"—"I need a *friend*."

"Sure," Bern had said, wondering where the opening lay in this genteel arrangement. There was always an opening. Her solicitude had tempered his fears of unseemliness. He could be patient. In a shockingly short time, he had learned to depend on her company, as he had formerly staked his comfort on his solitude.

Now, today, on Fifth Avenue, anticipating supper with Kate at the Cedar (Gary—whom Bern had not yet met—had a late evening at the theater, with rehearsals for a new play), Bern reflected on how his renewal had arrived: not with the Ann Cline book or his sketches of huts, but from the conversations Kate tripped him into, the challenge of articulating his cherished principles to a person who had never heard them before. New people! Who knew?

He wished he could share his revival with the city. Apparently, post-9/11, the thirteenth century was "in" again. Barricades. Blocky walls. The old/new urban style. He thought once more of the Freedom Tower. The prismatic glass panels planned for its base couldn't hide the *flinch* in its frame. The other day in the office, one of Bern's young colleagues had joked that, in the age of expanding terrorism, architects required military training: "Mark my words. We're going to see Rem Koolhaas marching around Rockefeller Center in a helmet and a flak jacket."

If only the city had kept its *lightness*. Bern missed the "Phantom Towers," the twin beams of light cast into the sky from Ground Zero, six months after the shock: a powdery afterimage of what had once existed on the spot, and a public echo of the private vigils that had taken place with candles in every neighborhood. An architecture of the imagination.

He also missed the spirit of sober whimsy that had risen in the attack's immediate aftermath: for instance, the suggestion (who had made it—some artist?) that the barricades around the smoking pit be replaced by plastic piping—shifting, soft, ringed with buckets for flowers. Instead, burdened by habitual politics and the egos of celebrity architects, the site's fate had locked into a predictable pattern, with little hope of renewal.

Either way, Bern thought—vulnerability or an impregnability so forbidding even citizens felt imprisoned—suicide was the end result.

Perhaps, at this point, a giant marble head of Robert Moses was the most appropriate marker for the site. Vandal planners could sneak into the area at night, swords at the ready, zoning codes hand-printed on vellum clutched to their armored bosoms. Ritual dances could be aimed at cursing the mayor. Chanting, drumming, spray-painting Jane Jacobs's face on the Power Broker's pockmarked nose, a nose the size of a motorboat.

The city's many layers, like centuries of sand in a desert. If Bern had helped Kate bore into them, she had enabled him to tunnel back into and forgive himself his first reckless enthusiasms here: the art parties he'd been invited to on upper Broadway and in SoHo and Chelsea when he'd just arrived, a fresh young professional. For a few years he'd stayed active in the art scene, shyly attending openings, until the high energy of mingling with strangers finally wore him down.

He recalled Dan Flavin's wedding in the Guggenheim—'92? '91? A friend of a friend, a staffer with the Landmarks Preservation Commission, had gotten Bern an invitation to the gala because the artist's young bride, a painter, was a Texan. Bern's acquaintance thought he might know her, as if Texas were no bigger than a kitchen. The bride was stunning, tall and dark-haired in a shimmering white Isaac Mizrahi dress. All night, Bern skirted the edges of the ceremony.

He didn't long now for the awkwardness of grand public

occasions, preferring his sandwiches in the corners of quiet bars, but jogged by Kate's fondness for the city's tchotchkes he remembered the mystery and magic of certain moments. For Flavin's wedding the museum's inner walls were bathed with ultraviolet light, with yellows, pinks, and greens turning the corridors into rivers, the walls into warm energy. That night, Bern had felt that the building and everyone in it would lift into the air; he imagined the bride's dark hair grazing his face as they rose hand in hand into paradise, which smelled of blossoming moss roses.

The one blemish on Bern's private wall of remembrance was his ex-wife's unhappiness. Marla came from an old Houston family with conservative politics and narrow social values, yet she had always seemed easygoing and nonjudgmental—until New York. The prodigious drinking and sexual energy at art parties rattled her. She claimed she wasn't homophobic, yet Bern felt her stiffen in the presence of gays. Manhattan acted as a palette knife, scraping off the unfixed surface of her personality and revealing the coarser base underneath. A common enough story. But this isn't fair to her, Bern thought. Even in 1983, when she complained about the city's squalor, its noise and dirt and heat, its exorbitant prices—"Back home, for this rent, I could get the fucking Astrodome!"—he understood that deeper currents shocked her into smashing against her surroundings, and he may have been part of the problem. Just as the city's rhythms unlocked movements in her behavior that Bern hadn't sensed before, it unleashed his latent capacities for self-absorption, obsessive work, quiet anxiety. This much he had learned about himself in twenty years: whole swamps of his quirks remained hidden from him. He had known from the first that Marla didn't have patience for his pronouncements, not the way Kate did now.

What continuing part, if any, did Bern play in Marla's mental life? A few years ago, a friend informed him that her father had died, a gentle man whom Bern had always liked, and he had given her a brief condolence call. He hadn't spoken to her since then— over a decade now.

Remembrance. Hopeless.

Over the years since Marla's departure, he'd developed a reputation in the office as a loner, slightly off-kilter, seldom dating, seldom leaving early for the day. He worked hard, earning the firm a small, steady profit, so his job was secure. But the young guns (he was about their age when he started) with their software lingo, their gossip about Robert Venturi and postmodernism, viewed his passion for history, his "seeking the truth in building," as quaint. Behind his back (but not so softly he didn't hear it) they called him the "Utopian." In the coffee room, one of them would quip, "You know, Wally, eventually every utopian experiment ends in tyranny and disaster," and they'd all crack up. Bern thought it a serious point, worth pursuing.

What he really wanted to tell them, if they had granted him the courtesy of entertaining his ideas, was that he didn't care about Utopia. From his office window he could point to billboards, tenements, distant shipping cranes, sewer pipes exposed beneath jack-hammered sidewalks, the used clothing store. He could turn and ask his colleagues, if they had ever gathered in his office to listen (as he often imagined them doing—on a pleasant late afternoon, say, the sun in bright squares on his carpet, a lazy warmth in the room), "What do the things we see around us have to do with our inner lives? Is this blandness a reflection of who we are? Or do we come to reflect the objects we live among?"

But the original young guns had all moved up or out, leaving

Bern in the same old spot surrounded by fresh faces, men and women whose years he *did* now exceed. Considerably. The youngsters got the corner offices, the sexy commissions (trendy night spots, restaurants in Trump's benevolent shadow) while the nonprofits trickled down to Bern, the social service agencies in need of a bit more room, old churches looking to remodel, foundations with cash restrictions—projects for which a slow pace and a simple approach could still turn a profit for the firm, and earn Bern's bosses citizenship points throughout the community.

Lately, *function* was the firm's motivational catchword: workplace as System, with each component fulfilling its designated capacities. Bern understood function in more natural terms, as the *suffering of a process*, the way wood weathers over time, or the body experiences mild discomfort as it goes about its sweet digestive task.

He stood now facing St. Patrick's Cathedral. Shadows of birds moved lazily on the white marble arches. A man with a camera bumped his shoulder, mumbled "Sorry," and moved to take a picture of the church's shaded steps. The man said something in French to a female companion. Bern caught the words *sacre* and *cite*. *Sacre*, he thought he recalled from school, meant "cursed" as well as "holy."

He remembered reading, years ago on an airplane, a not-bad thriller about an IRA man who rigged the cathedral with bombs.

The church's treelike spires and gently bending portals reminded him of his moment with Kate the other night in front of the Presbyterian's arch. Mysterious groves, these houses of worship, forests encased in stone, hiding secret rituals. Wind wheezed in the gaps among the rose-colored windows. The breath of orphans, Bern thought, children now forgotten, whom monks once tended on this site, long before the cathedral was built. The structure's thin arcs resembled oak limbs laden with ornaments: animal skulls, pelts, and hides—the leavings of a sacrifice, the attempt to dress up murder as a thoughtful gift to the gods.

Bern shivered, the sunlight cold on his skin. A group of Japanese tourists joined the French couple in a digital snapfest. Bern turned. He didn't want to hurry back to the office, to the chatter of his young colleagues. Moving slowly down Fifth, he was startled to see a pair of homeless men kneeling under a makeshift shelter in the space between a clothier and a bank. Since Giuliani's Days of Stomp-and-Thunder, the homeless had become largely invisible in New York, especially in an area such as this. The men recalled recent photographs of post-Katrina New Orleans.

A shopping cart, cardboard, blue plastic tarp . . . but the squatters had also outfitted their space with metal buckets of differing sizes, and paper kites arranged to create an airy, split-level effect, almost Oriental in its aesthetic. Ingenious. While in grad school, as part of his dissertation project—an investigation into architectural origins—Bern had traveled to some of the world's political hotspots. Nicaragua, Yemen. He had witnessed brilliant adaptations of the "primitive" to the modern, to organic necessity, to cultural arrogance: in Managua, he had marveled at the marriage of native stone to Spanish colonialism, and in Sanaa, at the use of dun-colored mud in sheltering animals, children, and the elderly—but never, he decided now, as he admired what these men had done with their scraps, had he seen such elegant adaptability.

Dread. Bern thought, isn't that what drives construction—fear of harsh sunlight, wind storms, lightning? Honoring terror, a precondition for beauty, instead of trying to stave it off? One of the men shared with the other a slice of uncooked frozen pizza.

This spot, with an asking price of nearly $1,500 per square

foot, was, Bern knew, one of the most expensive strips of real estate on the planet.

He passed an IRS branch office. With each ticking second, an LED sign above its door counted off the size of the national debt. The numbers, in the trillions, flashed as quickly as the burps of a Geiger counter he remembered using in his middle school science class. One day, he had sat with twelve other sweaty kids in the center of a football field to measure the assault of the earth by solar rays.

On the north side of Union Square, Bern saw a billboard touting "Lifestyle Buildings." He didn't know what a "Lifestyle Building" was, and he experienced a moment of panic. Was it possible that eventually you lost your edge in the city? Dulled by overwork, so you couldn't even spot a wedge of geese?

When he reached the office he spoke to no one. Two of his colleagues argued in the hallway outside his door—something about a realtor "flipping a building, repping a new client." "We *all* know that product doesn't move that far south of the fucking park," said one of the men. "Everyone in America knows that!"

The wide glass doors of Bern's apartment building infused him with relief from half a block away. A quick change of shirts, a fresh tie before running to meet Kate. When he entered the lobby, he saw Mrs. Mehl sitting hunched and red-eyed on the sofa. Ryszard, the super, knelt beside her, dabbing her face with a wet cloth. Two tall blondes and a dark woman with taut, boxy hair (a look Bern associated with fashion magazines and stoned stupidity) stood in the center of the room. They held whippets on diamond-studded leashes. The dogs were gorgeous, vividly sculpted, gray with wispy orange streaks down their legs.

"I told him, 'Why shouldn't I style my personality after my pet?'" one of the blondes said to her companions. "Style is style, darling. You take it where you can get it."

Bern thought, No animals were harmed in the making of this psyche.

He nodded hello to Ryszard and asked Mrs. Mehl what had happened. She said she was taking her cat to the vet, making her way through the lobby when "these three harridans stomped in with their smelly old beasts and scared my little poopsie. She ran out the door."

"We should have known we had the wrong building," the dark woman said to her friends. "*Look* at this dump. Stephane would never stay here. He'd be ill."

"All right, all right," Ryszard grunted, waving his arms. No matter the concern—a burst pipe, a minor break-in, a scuffle in the elevator—from Ryszard it was "All right, all right" and a choppy wave of the arms. He was Polish, had never learned much English, couldn't repair a paper clip, yet somehow had earned the landlord's trust. He'd been a fixture in the building for years.

True, he was strangely effective in emergencies involving livid people. Bern figured this was because Ryszard's presence was such an anomaly; people backed off rather than engage a fellow with whom it was clear there would never be a resolution. He reminded Bern of a puffer fish he'd seen once in a wildlife documentary.

The whippets left the building, tugging the harridans behind them.

Ryszard pressed the wet cloth into Bern's hands and shuffled to the stairway. Bern helped Mrs. Mehl into the lift. She was the very image of reduced yet indomitable dignity, like the homeless men on the street. "I'll draw up some flyers. We'll post them around the block, and over at McGee's," he told her. "We'll find your cat." For once this week—the fire escape still nettled him—his drawing skills might be useful. Mrs. Mehl described the animal to Bern. "Her name is Madame Anna Mona Pasternak," she said. "After my aunt, in Minsk."

"That's unusual."

"It's her *name*."

"Yes, yes. Of course."

"Put it on the flyer."

"I will."

The old woman moved slowly down the third-floor hallway, and it occurred to Bern that she could pass away before they found her pet. He wouldn't be surprised to hear in the morning that she had died in her sleep. Well, he thought: life among others.

The phone in his living room blinked its round red eye. A message from Kate. The moment he heard her voice, he convinced himself she had called to cancel. "Wally, I walked by the Cedar today at lunch. It's closed!" she said. "There's a sign in the window saying the disruption is only temporary."

He stared at his moss rose. What was more distressing—the news about the Cedar or the insecurity Kate's voice had just caused him? Was he becoming too dependent on this girl?

"Why don't you come to my place?" Kate said.

Her place.

"I'll fix us some gumbo. A salty little taste of the Gulf, how's that? And Wally? I know what you're thinking."

Flame in his cheeks.

"You're thinking it's another loss—the Cedar."

His shoulders fell. Once again, his insecurities had forced him face to face with his vanity. Naturally, it didn't occur to Kate that her invitation would arouse him, even mildly. She didn't think about him the way he thought about her. Wasn't that clear by now?

"The sign *does* say 'Temporary,'" Kate observed. "Let's wait and see, okay? It doesn't mean the sky is falling again."

Sweet girl.

"I'll see you around six?" she said. The loud click of her hang-up echoed the ticking of the numbers on the national debt sign.

Bern pulled from his closet a fresh, white, long-sleeved shirt. Should he iron it? The collar was askew. Wouldn't ironing sug-gest—*reveal*—to Kate a hope on his part?

It's said that Carlo Lodoli was perpetually disheveled and dank, distracted as he moved through the world. Yet young people flocked around his tattered, tottering frame, eager to hear his talk.

In the bedroom, Bern considered his face in the mirror of his dresser. Querulous. Pale. An expression of frozen surprise. He recalled the lost eyes and mouths on the wall at St. Vincent's. Tucked inside the wooden edge of the frame around his mirror was a newspaper clipping, yellowed now, about the discovery of an old burial ground in Lower Manhattan. Workers had unearthed ten to twenty thousand slave remains when they dug a pit for a new fed-eral building. Bern had kept the clipping to keep alive in his mind knowledge of what Kate called the city's layers—the island's onion skins. Paper and bone. A passing breath.

The clipping nudged another scrap on the mirror, also begin-ning to yellow: "Ten Rules for Cardiovascular Health."

Bern's dresser was thick with relics from his past: a framed quote from an Isaac Babel story: "You Must Know Everything." Marla had given it to him for his twenty-eighth birthday. A cherrywood box for paper clips and pennies, also a gift from Marla. A comb, rarely used. An empty container for "Cactus Candy," a souvenir of

Houston, vividly blue and green with a hot yellow streak on the side of the box. Probably these things will outlast me, Bern thought. Through the years, their hard edges will soften but remain, and here they'll stay: testimony to the life I lived, good or ill.

Kate's place resembled a parochial school, with framed, out-of-register prints of St. Patrick and the Virgin on the wall above a bookshelf. On the shelf were candles in thick glass containers imprinted with the faces of saints and prayers for salvation, fortitude, and luck.

The solemn atmosphere, broken only by a couple of sports magazines left open on the floor, was bolstered by Faure's *Requiem*, playing softly on the CD player. Bern recognized the stately Kyrie.

In the lobby, on his way to the elevator, Bern had noticed the grime on the walls, the tiles like weak, malarial eyes staring at him. The stench of old cabbage and rotting meats in black plastic bags piled in a side room next to the elevator shaft caused his stomach to clench, the odors clashing with the scent of the single rose he'd brought for Kate. The feathery erotic charge that had tickled his skin since her phone message dissipated in the lobby's pungent assault.

The building's hallways appeared to be part of a wasp's nest, cells within cells. Rough, sandy walls. Holiday decorations—all out of season (red Christmas bells, cardboard skeletons, brittle and dry four-leaf clovers)—sagged on a few apartment doors.

When Kate let him in, her roses and the cayenne prickle of the soup carried him back into East Texas bayous: the hunt for crayfish in muddy bottomlands packed with steamy brown leaves, warm seepage from rice paddies.

"How nice," Kate said, taking the rose from his hand. She

placed it in a glass of water and set the glass on a wood plank atop her antique radiator, next to pots of roses. Starlike blossoms strained toward the window and the lights of the street. "Portaluca, the man at the market told me these were called," Kate said, touching the flowers. "I'd never heard that name. I guess that's what they say up here. Wine?"

"Yes, thanks," Bern said. Through her window he glimpsed satellite dishes, ash cans, rainspouts.

She pulled the cork from a bottle of Cabernet.

"No Guinness?" Bern asked.

"I only drink Guinness in bars, to impress older men," Kate said. She saw him eyeing the saints. "I know. It's like a K-Mart convent in here. I'm lapsed, don't worry. What can I say—I like the kitsch. It comforts me. Childhood, you know. You?"

He thought she meant the wine, to which he had already assented, and he stood puzzled. Then he realized she was asking about his religious upbringing.

"Oh. Nominally Jewish. What the newspapers call 'cultural Judaism.' Little to do with faith, so I never had a chance to lapse. I must say, I've noticed in others that 'lapsed' is a pretty murky category."

Kate laughed and raised a thick brown brow. "A Texas Jew . . ."

"It's true, we were rare in our part of Houston. But not ostentatious, which is why my wife's family, good Southern Baptists, finally accepted me in spite of their doubts."

"You married hellfire?"

"She told me she had lapsed."

"I see."

Now the *Requiem* soared. The minor strains of the Offertory gave way to the Sanctus. The violas wept.

Kate didn't join him in the wine. For herself she poured a glass of mineral water. He felt the odd treat of seeing her beyond public arenas, among her private things, at a rhythm of her choosing. He would watch. He would learn.

"Gumbo's almost ready," she told him. "Relax. *Mi casa es tu casa* . . . does that apply to rentals? Anyway, kick those magazines out of your way. Gary's old baseball stuff . . ."

At the mention of the name, Bern stiffened involuntarily. He stepped around the magazines as though they were predators whose sleep he shouldn't disturb. The wine tasted like pepper.

She ladled the gumbo into fat yellow bowls, topped off his glass of wine, and placed a stiff baguette, wrapped in a tea towel on a platter, on her tiny dining room table. She switched off the lights in the kitchen. Candlelight perked across her forehead, nose, and cheeks. They toasted. The *Requiem* reached its climax—in Paradisum. The piece's martial pacing opened up into lighthearted trills: for one jaunty measure, Bern caught something like a Rodgers and Hart beat. Perverse of him to hear, in sacred strains, the Great White Way. What kind of philistine was he? What was he doing here?

"—stereotypes," Kate was saying. "Two summers ago, in Northern Ireland—my first and only time there—and it was strange because I felt a pull from the place, given my family history and all, but I wondered how much I had talked myself into . . . you know, tourism and prefab nostalgia . . . and how much of my attraction was genuine? What did 'genuine' even mean?"

Bern watched her face and nodded as she spoke. He brought a spoonful of steaming soup to his mouth. "This is delicious," he said.

"Could have used more salt. Anyway," she said, rising, "what was I responding to? Some smell from the stones? The moss? The air? Were the genes stirring inside my body? Or was this feeling just bullshit, the magic of my Visa card?" She laughed, placing a new CD in her player. "Now for something *completely* different. Do you mind?" A computerized thudding imploded in her speakers.

"Not at all," Bern said.

"Death Cab for Cutie," Kate said, tapping the CD case. "I just discovered them. But Ireland. It was weird, Wally, because *my* family's experience wasn't the happy-go-lucky . . . you know . . . drunken revelry, storytelling, that sort of thing. The O'Dochertaighs—my ancient relatives—were the last of Donegal's seventeenth-century clan lords. The summer I visited, I'd drive my rental car into some village on the coast, stop and ask directions, talk to folks. When they found out I was an O'Dochertaigh, their faces crumpled. 'Ah God,' they'd say, 'not another one.' They'd squint at me: 'Yes, yes, you'd fit in any ditch around here.' I mean, four hundred years had passed, and *still* the O'Dochertaigh name was associated with brutality and war."

"Pleasant group, your folks. Available for weddings, wakes, and plunder."

"In a pub one night, a nice old gent even suggested to me, gently, politely, but *still*, that the O'Dochertaighs were just like the Israeli army, occupying Gaza. And this was *centuries* ago!"

"Well, but look what's happening now in Belfast," Bern said. "Gerry Adams and Ian Paisley breaking bread together. Unthinkable, right, even a few years ago."

"Yes, it's confusing," Kate said. "Incredibly hopeful, on the one hand, and on the other . . . you should have seen Derry, Wally. So moving. The 'Free Derry' murals at the Bogside, commemorating the Bloody Sunday martyrs. But there again, someone had come along and spray-painted pro-Palestinian graffiti across several of the pictures. Like there was no difference between . . . ah hell . . ."

She laughed. Her cheeks had flushed with excitement, the color of warm copper, a color Bern wanted to touch, the way he often felt compelled to run his hand along smooth staircase banisters in vintage buildings—the slow, comforting ascent, a retreat from the world outside.

"I'm one to talk," Kate said. "One of my ancestors, a warlord named Cahir, sacked Derry in 1608—a deliberate provocation of the British. He burned the place to the ground. So that's *my* family's legacy. Great, right? I've got the death of a city on my conscience, and the people there won't let me forget it!" She laughed again.

"What if I designed a hut for you?" Bern said. "'The Atonement Hut.' You could offer it to the Derry city council . . ."

Kate smiled but her mood had slipped. "Wally?"

"Yes?"

"Do you think we'll ever get over it?"

He searched her eyes.

"You know."

He had splattered soup on his shirt. He dabbed the spot with his napkin. "Naturally, certain individuals will never get over it," he said. "But it seems to me that—except for the site itself—the city has moved on, for the most part. Doesn't it seem so to you?"

"Yes. I guess. But—*should* we move on? Maybe *that's* what I'm asking."

"Ah."

"I mean, I know we have to. Sort of. But your hut—isn't it—"

Bern slid his hand toward hers—aware of the stain on his shirt, of the sweet smell of roses in the room. "Kate. By any chance, is this about New Orleans?"

"I don't know," she said. "I—"

"Maybe you should go back and see it. You still have friends there, right? Places that meant a lot to you?"

"Yes."

"I'm not a believer in 'closure,'" Bern said. "But I do trust reconnecting. Grounding oneself. When you told me you hadn't been back since the storm, I confess I was shocked."

"First principles."

"Yes."

She removed her hand from his. "Well, this is awfully gloomy talk for such a lovely evening. I'm sorry. How did we get into all that? I was telling you about my family, my trip to Ireland . . ." She refilled his wine glass.

"Will you join me?" Bern said. "I can't drink the whole bottle."

"I shouldn't." She wrinkled her nose. A little girl's face: an attempt to pass off as trivial something quite serious. Bern sensed this immediately. "It's annoying, and I can't believe myself," Kate said rapidly, her eyes full of reflected candle flames. The room's low light and its shadows made her face fluid, her nose and lips like the tips of underwater reeds, now foreshortened, now elongated as the candles flickered. "This morning I realized . . . I think I'm pregnant," she said. "Pure carelessness. I haven't told Gary, not until I'm absolutely certain, and he's going to . . . Wally? Wally, what is it?"

She stared at him as though she feared his heart had seized up. And his heartbeat *did* quicken, surprising him.

"It's nothing, really. Just a little morning sickness," Kate said, responding to his question.

Bern wiped his mouth and stood. He walked over to the bookshelves. Dizzy. The wine. The roses. He studied the face of a saint on one of the tall glass candleholders: an androgynous, childlike figure in a blue-plumed hat, with brown curly hair, dark eyes, and a rose-petal mouth. The saint, seated on a wooden throne, held a basket and a golden staff. "The Holy Child of Atocha," said a paper label on the glass. "Purify our hearts by the example of your meekness."

He turned to Kate. Though she sat in shadow, he saw that she had registered what surely marked his face. Sexual jealousy. A man of his age! Yes, yes: he was a pathetic gag gift at someone else's party. A trick can of peanuts . . . pop the lid . . . the fake, ungainly snake.

"Oh shit," Kate said.

Bern stared at his shoes: smeared with the dirt of the streets.

Kate carried the yellow soup bowls to her tiny kitchen sink. Death Cab shook the room. The flowers trembled. "I thought we . . . I thought you understood," Kate said.

"Yes," Bern said.

"But?"

"But."

She whirled to face him, her wet, soapy hands on her hips. "Can we get around this, Wally? I really enjoy our friendship."

Her words sent heat through his arms. Kate glanced at his face, and he wanted to hide. "Do you . . . ," he said. "Excuse me, "I need to tidy up this stain, where is you-your . . ."

"Down the hall. To your left," she said tersely.

She didn't have a hallway. He stood rooted, a disoriented clown. Then he remembered that, on each floor of this old building, three or four units shared a single bath. She meant the hallway outside her apartment.

Architecture.

He walked to the door.

Institutional green tiles lined the bathroom walls. A toilet and a shower missing its curtain filled the minuscule space. Someone had left a plastic bag stuffed with pink soap and a hair net hanging by a cord from the shower nozzle. The nozzle dripped black water. The toilet bowl was plugged with shit and enough paper to fill a Brooklyn phone book.

His vision blurred. His shirt stain seemed to spread, like the smell in the room. He tore off a piece of toilet paper and wiped his slick forehead. His stomach pitched. He took slow breaths until his pulse returned to normal.

By the time he got back to Kate's living room, rage coiled in the muscles of his arms, though he couldn't locate its source. She stood in the kitchen where he'd left her, drying her hands on a towel. A sting of pepper in the air. The gumbo. His eyes watered. A smell of smoke. One of the candles had guttered.

Kate wouldn't look at him. "I'm sorry, Wally. Maybe it's not possible to . . . I mean, for a man, a man who's been lonely for a while, and a young woman—"

"It's possible, Kate. We'll do it, okay?" He knew his words sounded harsh. He had no control. "It's just that, I didn't picture myself babysitting some young couple as they worked out their little soap opera . . ."

Mistake, he thought. Erase. Erase.

"Babysit?" Kate said.

"You're right. I'm feeling sorry for myself. I shouldn't . . ." Act your age, old fool. Tighten the screws. "I apologize."

Kate crossed her arms over her breasts. The dish towel hung from one of her hands and covered her torso, demurely. "I think you should go, Wally."

He made a formal bow. A bobbing punch-clown. "I'm sorry, Kate."

"I'm sorry, too."

"Thank you for dinner."

She nodded.

Only steps away from Kate's he felt his shoe crack—a slapstick flapping of the worn right heel—as he crossed Seventh where, apparently, the new St. Vincent's would be built. Bern went through shoes at an alarming rate: three pairs in the last six months. Shoddy craftsmanship, he thought. Then: Of course she doesn't want me. I'm just an old curmudgeon.

In the middle of the avenue, a crumpled Starbucks cup blew against his instep.

His heart beat fast again. His hands smelled of salt and cayenne, and faintly of the flower he'd cut for Kate.

The western sky was glass streaked violet with a smear of orange. From the shadows of the hospital a dirty, khaki-clad figure reeking of gin and onions lurched at a pair of girls. "Cigarette," he said. "Fuckface. Fuckface." The girls fell back against a wall. Bern thought of stepping in—but why? To do what? Assert himself? At his age? These girls were old enough to stroll around the city on their own, to cope with whatever the streets tossed up at them. One of the young ladies fished a cigarette from her purse.

Bern started to head up Seventh toward a subway station. On Kate's corner, a raucous party erupted out of a brownstone's doorway, down the building's concrete steps. Young people laughing and drinking beer from silver cans. Many of them appeared to be interns at St. Vincent's—they wore wrinkled green medical smocks. A basket of blue paper slippers, the kind doctors pull over their shoes for sanitary purposes, stood on the stoop. The revelers seemed to be using the slippers as party favors, wearing them on their heads or hands, or stuffing them into their pockets so they resembled boutonnieres. Inside, the crowd danced to laborious hip-hop, while dressed to treat gunshot wounds, burns, and lacerations.

Bern glanced back one last time at Kate's place. Would she let him in now if he showed up, hangdog? Probably she was in bed. He veered away and, thinking of her, missed the subway station. Well, it felt good to walk. It always felt good to walk. His shoe heel clattered on the street like the ceramic tiles hung on a chain-link fence, three or four blocks back, commemorating 9/11. The tiles came from New York well-wishers: "Ohio Is Thinking of You!" "Arizona Says God Bless NYC!" When wind blew and shook the fence, the tiles rattled like seed-filled gourds.

Tomorrow he would telephone Kate. Yes. He was the mature one here: it was up to him to make things right. They *would* forge a friendship, by God—against all odds. Men and women: it could be done. Belfast, right?

Don't get carried away, Bern told himself immediately. After all, "making things right" meant taking small steps. Building a hut one mud brick, one pole, at a time. An apology. A design for a fire escape. A poster for a missing cat. He had learned his lessons from Lodoli, had *become* Lodoli, watching the great cities of his time wax and wane, and wax again. Live lightly on the earth, he thought, and leave all pages blank.

On a sidewalk grating Bern paused impulsively, then steadied his feet as a subway train thundered beneath him.

Wendy Madar

TRACY DAUGHERTY

is the author of four novels, three previous short story collections, and a
book of personal essays. *Hiding Man*,
his biography of Donald Barthelme,
was published in 2009. He has received
fellowships from the Guggenheim
Foundation, the National Endowment
for the Arts, and the Vermont Studio
Center. A member of the Texas Institute of Letters, he is a four-time
winner of the Oregon Book Award. Currently, he is Distinguished
Professor of English and Creative Writing at Oregon State University.